D0869699

DIRT BAG

SOLE SURVIVOR

KHATARI

Published by: Neva Die Publications

This is a work of fiction. Names, characters, businesses, places, events, and incidents are either the products of the author's imagination or used in a fictitious manner.

Any resemblance to actual persons, living or dead, or actual events is purely coincidental.

PRAYER

Heavenly father, you've blessed me with many talents, gifts and I thank you for them. Perhaps one of the greatest you have ever given me is the ability to reach and move others. For many moons, this gift has been wasted, used negatively and for all the wrong reasons. Yet you were patient with me, forgiving and understanding. For you knew one day that I would come to grips with reality, open my eyes, and wake up....... That day is at hand!!

I now see things clearly because my oculars are finally opened. My spiritual eyes now see. I see reality, not as it is, but as it should have been all along and the truth behind it. I will no longer abuse or take for granted the many talents you have given me. I shall use my attributes to help the masses open their eyes and see what they have been missing. To accept that which they have feared and to embrace what is to come. Within every story lies the truth, and that truth is the meaning of life. To live and experience, in hopes that we learn from our experiences and learn from our mistakes.

Father I have learned!!!!!

AMEN!!

DEDICATION

This book is dedicated to all the Dirt Bags out there. The little lost, scared, and abandoned souls that life, society, and others have forgotten about. My name is Khatari, and I'll never forget you because I am you. I will never forget the pain of the abuse. The neglect, hurt, and fear. Nor shall I ever fully recover from the self- doubt and hatred caused by that abuse. Even now as I am writing this, I still ask myself how could someone do so many evil things to a child? At time, it appears, that some questions will never be answered. All that is left, is for us to help one another outgrow the situation and move on. Although we will never outgrow the pain, we must remember it only exist as a memory in our mind. If you ignore it long enough you will eventually forget it.

KHATARI (The Dragon)!!

SYNOPSIS

After being kidnapped by a psychopath with multiple personality disorder, young Thomas Smith Jr. aka Lolo was in a fight for his life.

During Lolo's captivity, a twisted tale began to unfold. A tale of murder, tragedy, love, and a fight for survival that began three years earlier when his mother revealed that she was not his biological mother while on her death bed, as well as revealing to him that he was the son of the infamous She-Wolf, Anne, and the legendary Mobb Boss, Thomas T'Rida Smith.

After his mom's death, he found himself homeless, doing any and everything he could, to ensure his survival. Along the way, he met Nyomi, another lost soul and fell in love. A love that would be taken away when tragedy strikes again.

This is an epic, captivating, on the edge of your seat thriller about the many misfortunes that led to Lolo turning into the legendary Dirt Bag.

CHAPTER ONE

The night sky erupted violently as the war between
lightning and thunder waged on. Sporadic white lights brought
an eerie contrast to the sky's pitch-black void. The wind blew a
mighty sixty-five miles an hour gust that screamed and howled
like wild beast terrorizing the haunted forest of Winchester.
Raindrops the size of quarters sounded like hollow point
bullets as they crashed and pelted the black rubber covers of
the BFI garbage dumpster.

This was the type of storm that made horror movies
scary as hell. This wasn't a movie though; this was real life.
The mighty storm was called "El Nino", and it was fierce and
raging. Mass flooding and flash floods have been destroying
the streets and highways of California's Bay Area for days now
and there was no sign of the storm letting up any time soon!

Inside of the dumpster buried deep down below all the
filth and garbage, trembling, and shivering from the frigid cold
is little ten-year-old Thomas Smith, aka Lolo. Even with the
garbage lid closed a few gallons of water had managed to
somehow find a way to seep in, saturating the garbage and
debris.

Of course, being surrounded by soaking wet trash has
caused his clothes to become soaking wet as well. Lolo tried
desperately to keep his tiny teeth from chattering, but it was a
battle that he continues to lose. Mentally he kicked himself in
the ass for getting caught in the storm this far away from his
little hideout. Had he made it back to the hideout before the
storm started up again, he would be dry and warm right now.

Instead, he miscalculated the breaks in between the
downpours and now he was paying the price. For the tenth
time, Lolo contemplated leaving the dumpster to search for a
better place to spend the night and escape the fearsome storm.
The problem with that was the reason he decided not to leave
the other nine times. Lolo was only eighty-five pounds with

10

boots on and quarters in his pocket. Unless he travelled in the same direction the wind was blowing, it would constantly knock him on his ass. Still, he told himself that at least there would be comfort at the end of his suffering. The question was, how much longer would it be before he found shelter.

Something stirred next to him, stealing his attention. It was a subtle move, but he felt it, nevertheless. He focused in on the area where he thought it came from.

Again, there it was. This time there was more movement.

Lolo's tiny heart began to beat rapidly as fear began to replace his discomfort. He sat there, still as could be, until he heard the squeaking sound of an enormous rat.

Fuck the storm!

Lolo threw caution to the wind and bolted out of the dumpster. He would rather be drenched and freeze to death than to get bitten by a filthy rat.

His little brain could not absorb all the abuse that he was taking and still function anywhere near its normal capacity. Because of this, Lolo wandered down the empty parking lot, behind the Mexican supermarket and taco shack on Willow Road.

His legs were beyond numb. He couldn't feel the ground beneath him, yet he struggled on. Suffering and pain were not strangers to Lolo. He knew them two muthafuckas all too well. After all he'd been homeless on the streets of the East Palo Alto and East Menlo Park for two years now.

As he reached Newbridge Street, the wind switched directions blowing mightily towards the northeast. Lolo didn't have the energy to fight the wind even if he wanted to. Instead, he half stumbled, and half slid down Newbridge headed towards Carlton Avenue.

The wind kicked up even stronger knocking him off balance. It felt like a car slammed into him when he hit the ground. Sharp needle like pains electrified his nerve endings throughout his body.

11

"Fuck!" his little voice screamed in his head. He wanted to give up. Say fuck it and die right here.

His mind flashed back to a time when his mother told him that God was always watching over him. She told him that God would always protect him from the evil devils of this world.

"Well, if God was watching over him and protecting him, then, where was he?" His poor little mind wondered.

Lolo couldn't wait on a God that he couldn't see. A God that has never came before, fuck that!

Somehow, he managed to pick himself up. The wind must've carried him because somehow he ended up a ways down on Carlton Avenue. He didn't remember ever turning the corner, let alone walking down the street.

He blinked his eyes, attempting to gather his bearings.

He was standing in front of a two-story, brown, and yellow house. The lights were on and shining through the windows on the second floor. How he longed to be inside the warm comforts of the house right then. Movement out of the corner of his eye drew his attention to the side of the house. A large cardboard box was between two garbage cans. One of the box's flaps came loose and was blowing back and forth. That's what caught his attention.

Lolo didn't believe the box was wet because the awning attached to the roof covered nearly the entire box. Thunder roared angrily, followed immediately by a lighting display that lasted ten full seconds.

Lolo took that as a sign. Making up his mind he should hide under the cardboard instead of continuing down the street.

He lifted the hatch to the fence. The wind covered any sound the latch made as well as the gate as he opened it. Inside the yard he paused momentarily to look up at the windows. The light in one of the windows went out. He wondered if someone saw him. Fear paralyzed him. He stood still while his heart raced.

A full minute later he figured if someone had saw him, they would've opened the front door by now. Again, thunder sounded. In his mind it was telling him to move. He made sure not to bump into anything as he made his way toward the side of the house. When he got there Lolo realized the cardboard box was one of those huge Home Depot moving boxes. His assumption was right. The box was as dry as it would be on a sunny, June day. He tilted the box over on its side and climbed in.

For the first time in a long time, he was happy. Not only did the box keep out the water, but it blocked the wind as well so that his wet clothes no longer felt so bad. Finally, he would be able to get some sleep. His poor body needed it.

Before long he dozed off and was sound asleep, dreaming of happier times. Times when his mother was alive. Even then life was shitty, but they had each other to help them get through it. Now it was just him. He didn't have any other family or loved ones to help him get through the fucked-up perils of life.

Suddenly, he was awakened.

He knew it couldn't have been morning already. Something was wrong, he could feel it. Tilting his head so that he could hear better. Lolo wondered what woke him up. Maybe it was the thunder. Who was he fooling? The thunder would not have bothered him. Something was wrong.

It didn't take long for Lolo to decide to leave. He'd learned a lot after being on his own living on the streets for two years. One of the most important lessons that he learned the hard way was never allow yourself to become a sitting target. Why? Because that was the easiest target to hit.

Lolo held his breath, so he could hear better as he slowly crawled to the front of the box. As he prepared to stick his head out to look around all the hairs on his body stood up. He ignored them, thinking it was just his nerves.

Slowly, he stuck his head out of the box. Nothing. He looked around as best he could but still didn't see anything. His clothes were still soaking wet which confirmed he hadn't been in the box that long.

Finally, he pulled himself all the way out of the box and stood listening to the storm. The battle raging on between thunder and lightning.

The hairs on the back of his neck stood up again. This time he could sense something or someone close by. He braced himself and turned around ready to confront whatever or whoever it was.

The dark night gave way to nothingness as something violently crashed into the side of his face. Lolo's unconscious body fell to the cold wet pavement!

CHAPTER TWO

Mama Terry Jennings just finished washing the dishes and cleaning up the kitchen after eating dinner. She made sure every single night that her house was cleaned before going to bed. She hated waking up in the morning to a filthy house. The sight alone would mess up her entire day.

"Yes, Jesus loves me. Yes, Jesus Loves me. Yes, Jesus Loves me. The Bible tells me so." She sung the old church hymn out loud as she made her way up the stairs to her room.

Lord, she was tired. She passed by the door to his room and momentarily thought about saying something to Terrence. Really, she didn't feel like dealing with him and his devil-some mouth. She was too tired for that.

Humming her church hymn to herself, she made her way to her room. Once inside she sat down on the bed and took a deep breath.

At 6'2", 240 pounds, Mama Terry was a very large woman. Years of labor have caused her shoulders to slouch and her back to bend. Though she moved around a lot slower than she used to when she was younger, she was still very much as strong as she used to be.

"The righteous eateth to the satisfying of his soul; but the belly of the wicked shall want." All day long she quoted Proverbs from the Bible.

She considered herself a devoted Christian, but her son Terrence was the Spawn of Satan. She never understood how something so vile came out of her womb.

The beeping sound of the motion detector connected to the front gate alerted her that an intruder just opened her front gate.

"Terrence! Someone opened the gate!" She called out to her son.

16

When he didn't answer, she called out to him again. "Terrence!"

"What?" Finally, he yelled back.

"Go check outside. We have an intruder." She yelled. "It's probably just the wind. Go to sleep, you old hag!"

Terrence was full after eating his dinner and tired. The last thing he wanted to do was go out into the cold, wet storm.

"Honor thy Mother and thy Father so thou days art longer!

Do as I tell you boy, and don't make me repeat myself." The tone of her voice dared him to test her.

"Alright, alright! Fuck! I'm going!" Terrence called out. Then he mumbled under his breath. "Old miserable fucking goat."

He grabbed the remote control and turned on the video monitor just in time to catch a small glimpse of someone walking around the corner of the side of the house.

"Stupid, fucking cocksucker. You picked the wrong fucking house to try and break into tonight." Terrence was excited as he grabbed his rusty aluminum baseball bat from the side of his nightstand.

His rain slicker was hanging on the back of the door. He grabbed it on his way out and put it on as he walked.

Terrence decided to take the back door instead of the front door due to the motion light that covered the front porch. It would automatically turn on the porch light which would alert the intruder. As silent as death, he slipped out of the back door and down the steps. The wind blew ferociously as the rain assaulted his rain slicker.

His rain slicker was floor length with a hood, and it was all black. The aluminum bat was tucked in his slicker.

Terrence was virtually invisible in the darkness of night. He stood still while his eyes surveyed the back yard looking for anything out of place.

Warm, hot blood raced through his veins as adrenaline sped up his heart rate. Oh, how he loved the thrill of the hunt. Standing a towering 6'2" and weighing 240 pounds of pure muscle. Whoever it is in his yard didn't stand a chance.

No one was in the back yard.

With the stealth of a jungle jaguar, he made his way over to the side of the house. The only thing he found once he got there was one of his moving boxes turned over onto its side.

Goddammit!" He wasn't paying attention to where he was going and knocked over an old gas can. So much for the element of surprise.

If somebody was out there, they most definitely heard that. To his surprise and delight something inside of the box stirred. Terrence was not above having fun at the expense of an animal. He had hoped it was a human. Nevertheless, he would not be denied his fun!

He crept up to the box on sound suppressant paws, masked as feet. Waiting patiently. The box moved again. It probably was a dumb stray dog, he told himself. Terrence licked his lips. His hot tongue felt like fire as it slid across dry, cracked lips. Suddenly the moment of truth arrived. Something was coming out of the box.

"Oh shit!"

It was human. A tiny something, but it was definitely human. Once it stood up, Terrence realized it was a child. He could feel himself becoming excited down there. Terrence had a sick fetish for little boys and girls. Especially, little boys. He bit down on his bottom lip. In his sick and perverse mind, he could taste his victim already.

The little child tensed up. It was at that moment Terrence realized his victim was aware of his presence. So, he prepared to capture his victim.

The child turned around and when he did so, Terrence swung his fist and hit him.

Terrence made sure to take some of the zap out of the punch considering how small the child was. His fist connected with the side of the child's head. In that split moment, he was able to tell it was a little boy. The poor fella dropped like a 50-pound sack of Idaho potatoes. "Yes! Yes! Yes!" Terrence began dancing around like a six-year-old kid, bouncing up and down as he excitedly chanted.

He stooped down and picked the little boy up, who couldn't weigh much more than an actual sack of potatoes. He carried the little boy on one shoulder making his way back inside the house. Even though the boy was knocked out Terrence still crept silently. He did not want his nosy ass mother to know about the little boy.

This was his little treat. He would not let her ruin it this time. Her with her fanatic, religious mumbo jumbo crap! What the fuck did she know about some God? Terrence knew her secrets. She was not as holy as she wanted to be.

He took the little boy down to the basement to secure him. The old hag did not come down to the basement, it was his personal playroom. The entire basement was soundproof to keep the nosy neighbors out of his business and he possessed the only key to the soundproof door or at least he thought so.

Terrence took the wet clothes off the little boy. The child was so malnourished that Terrence felt bad for him. He gazed over his little body with mixed emotions. Lust waged a battle against pity. He reached out to stroke the boy's shoulder but stopped midway. His hand hovered inches away from the boy's flesh. Pity won the battle. He dropped his hand back down to his side. For now, at least, pity had won out.

Terrence stood up and went and grabbed a warm blanket.

He draped the blanket over the little boy and prepared to leave, locking the door to the basement as he left. He slammed the back door as if he just came back into the house.

"What was it, Terrence?" his mother called out.

"It was nothing! I told yo' old ass the wind blew the gate open! Go to bed!" Fuck, the old bitch got on his last nerve. "Why don't she die already?" he mumbled.

"What took you so long then?" She continued to push.

"None of your fucking business! Fuck!" By now he had reached the stairs and was headed to his room.

CHAPTER THREE

Lolo slowly began to wake. When he tried to open his eyes, his head felt like it would cave in. He whined and moaned out loud. Where was he? All he could remember about last night was the terrible storm.

After the fifth attempt he was able to open his eyes. The level of pain was just tolerable enough to keep his eyes open. He knew he was inside some type of room. All he could see was an empty metal urine pan. The walls were barren. The air was stale and cold. Old, rusted pipes ran across the ceiling. As his eyes became stronger, he was able to make out a hot water heater in the corner. He remembered the hot water heater at their house. It was in the basement. That's it, apparently, he was in a basement. But how? Whose basement was he in?

A thousand thoughts ran through his mind at once. None of them were pleasant. There was no answer that he could come up with as to whose basement he was in that would set his mind at ease.

He had to get up. When he attempted to stand up, that was the first time that he felt the collar shackle that was around his neck.

Okay, now he knew the situation wasn't good. A fucking shackle around his neck, really? He was worried, but he knew that he couldn't panic. If he panicked, it would only make his situation worse. He needed to keep a level head and focus.

"There's always a way out of any situation." His mother used to tell him.

"All you have to do is stay levelheaded and think."

Lolo could hear Jennifer's voice in his ears like she was right there with him in that basement.

Adrenaline gave him the strength he needed to sit fully up in the bed. His head still pounded like a marching drum. Blinking his eyes, he fought off a bout of nausea. Once his stomach settled, his hands shot up toward his neck. Little, shaky fingers did everything they could do, desperately trying to see if by chance he could get the collar off.

Attached to the back of the collar was a fifteen-foot chain that was bolted to a stud in the wall. He tugged on the chain just to check it. Even if it hadn't been bolted in a stud, his puny little arms wouldn't even have been able to pull the chain out of the sheetrock.

Feeling defeated, he dropped the chain and sat on the bed. From the angle where he was seated, now he could see the entire room. To his left, was a cheap wooden nightstand. A plate of food was sitting on top of it. Next to the plate was a bowl full of something. Next to that was a TV remote. Across the room towards the left was an old woodworking station. It ran the length of the far wall. The stairs were over in the left corner. Directly in front of him was a TV sitting on a cabinet.

Apparently from the TV and the food, whoever had him, wanted him to get comfortable. Speaking of food, his stomach roared like a lion reminding him how hungry he was. He looked over at the plate again. It was loaded with fried chicken, rice covered in gravy, macaroni and cheese, and two big buttery Hungry Jack looking biscuits. The bowl was full of meaty homemade chili.

Lolo didn't waste any time; he snatched the plate up and went to town. Within minutes the only thing left on the plate was his saliva from licking the plate clean and the chicken bones. After letting out a loud burp, he grabbed the bowl of chili and knocked a patch out its ass too.

Now that he took care of business, he picked up the remote control and turned the TV on. The look of contentment that was on his face immediately disappeared the moment he laid eyes on what was on the screen. It was a porno movie.

The scene was of two women and one dude. He had one of the women doggy style pounding the shit out of her while her face was buried between the other woman's legs.

Why would there be a pornographic movie inside the video player waiting for him to turn it on? All types of bad thoughts swam through his mind.

Lolo pressed the button and turned the TV off. The feeling of doom overcame him again. Suddenly he felt vulnerable as for the first time he took notice of his nakedness.

It made sense now, whoever had him chained to the bed wanted him to stay a while because they were a fucking pervert. His little mind could only imagine what kind of sick twisted fuck had him held captive.

Lolo knew without a shadow of a doubt that he had to get the fuck up out of there. He may have only been ten, but he was far from a stupid little boy. He wasn't about to allow himself to be someone's sex slave.

Fuck that!

For some reason, his eyes became heavy. Just that fast he was very tired. When the room began swimming, he decided to lay down and rest his eyes for a second. Hopefully, that would help clear his head so he could think. The last thing little Lolo remembered was wondering what was there to think about.

Just like that, he was out cold.

**** N. D. ****

Lolo awakened to the delicious smell of hot food. His little mouth began to water due to the amazing aroma coming from the nightstand.

When he opened his eyes, a new plate lay before him on the nightstand full of food. He sat up and snatched the plate off the nightstand.

The first thing he shoved into his mouth was one of the smothered pork chops. There was a heaping pile of broccoli covered in cheese and two Hawaiian sweet dinner rolls, which sat on top of a pile of rice and gravy.

The food was amazing. Lolo had become so accustomed to surviving off whatever scraps and leftovers that he could find inside of the dumpsters of restaurants. Most of the time that was day old, stale stuff. He'd forgotten what homemade food tasted like.

He put a mountain size scoop of the rice into his mouth as he looked back over to the nightstand. There was a large cup of something sitting there.

Lolo knew he had been drugged earlier, and the chances were that he was being drugged again. But eventually the drug would wear off. Right now, he needed nutrients. In the past four days all he found to eat was half of a burrito someone gotten from the taco truck and a piece of a stale bagel.

He reached for the big blue plastic cup when suddenly, the hairs on the back of his neck stood up and goosebumps ran up his arm.

Lolo froze instantly on the spot. He was so engrossed with the food that he hadn't paid any attention to anything else.

Suddenly, he vaguely heard the sound of uttered words that appeared to be a man's voice. Lolo snapped his head to the right side of the room where the voice emerged.

It was a thick heavy voice laced with a raspy undertone.

Lolo didn't say anything. Fear caused his body to shake as he desperately tried to see in the poorly lit room.

"There's nothing for you to worry about little one. You're okay."

25

"I—If—If everything's okay, then why are you hiding?" The fear was easily picked up in his young voice.

"I'm not hiding. I just didn't want to disturb you while you were eating." The voice explained in a low whisper like tone.

"Who are you? What do you want?" Lolo's emotions were starting to get the best of him.

"I-I just wanna be your friend." Now the voice sounded light and high-pitched like a child.

"Who are you? Let me go! I don't wanna be your friend, I wanna go!" Lolo was in a full panic mode now. He was yelling and starting to cry.

"No. No. No!" It began as a small chant and grew to a raging roar.

"No! You can't leave! You're not going anywhere!"

The rage with which he yelled was frightful enough to silence little Lolo. If his voice didn't do it, the speed in which he shot out of the darkness and slapped the plate of food out of Lolo's hand surely did.

"You ungrateful little shit!" He slapped Lolo hard across the face!

"I take you out of the fucking storm! I cook and feed yo little funky ass and you wanna leave! No! No! NO!" He turned around and stormed over to the stairs and out of the basement.

Lolo stayed there trembling violently from fear. Paralyzed with shock, he could not move.

At ten years old he was smart enough not to believe in fairy- tales, but what he just saw had to be a monster. The guy was by far the biggest person Lolo had ever seen in his life. The speed in which he moved was indescribably fast. To add to that, he possessed the most hideous face imaginable.

He hadn't realized he used the bathroom on himself until the sheets became cold. He was too scared to be embarrassed and too shocked to move and do something about it.

**** N. D. ****

Mama Terry sat in her recliner in her room. Bebe and CeCe Winans played softly over the speakers while she read over her Bible.

"That demon child. Lord, please help him for he knows not what he does, Father." She was now looking up to the sky." Your word, Lord says the wages of sin is death. And Heaven knows that boy is constantly sinning. Lord, Church!"

"I don't know where that boy went wrong, Father! Lord knows I don't. His Daddy was a good man. A Godfearing man! Yes, he was. I just don't know about him Lord. He talks to me so disrespectfully. With such foul language. And he thinks I'm stupid. He does, doesn't he. Constantly going in and out of the basement at all hours of the day and night. He thinks I'm stupid, but I know!" Every time Mama Terry gets herself riled up; she begins shouting.

This behavior wasn't new. Mama Terry wasn't a millennium Christian like today's folk. No! She was old school, fire, and brimstone, old faith Christian. She didn't play with God and didn't like it when others did either.

"Do you not know that the unrighteous will not inherit the Kingdom of God? Do not be deceived. Neither fornicators, nor idolaters, nor adulterers, nor homosexuals, nor sodomites! Get thee behind me Satan! Back! Back, I tell you. Devil, get back!" She stood up and sat her Bible on the dresser.

Her sturdy paddle was on the side of the dresser where it always was. First, she grabbed a pair of scissors out of one of her drawers. Then she picked up the paddle.

She knew Terrence wasn't home. She hadn't heard him moving around in twenty minutes or so.

She headed to the basement. As she descended the stairs, she kept reciting Bible scriptures to herself.

"Flee sexual immorality. Every sin that a man does is outside the body, be he who commits sexual immorality sins against his own body."

She sat her paddle on the floor, leaned against the wall, once she made it to the door leading to the basement.

"Think I'm stupid do ya?" She stuck one of the legs of the scissors inside of the keyhole.

Next, she pushed down and twisted her wrist. Just like that the door unlocked.

Mama Terry then retrieved her sturdy paddle. It was one of those two-feet long wooden paddles about two inches thick, that resembled a rowing oar. Teachers used to have them back in the day before child services got involved.

Mama Terry was from a day and time when the classroom teacher had full rights and authority to paddle the behind of any troublemaker or disruptive child.

As she continued down the stairs, her heart was hoping that she was wrong. Yet, her mind told her she knew that she wasn't. The basement was dim, the air was thick and smelled rancid. As she reached the lower steps the strong stench of urine assaulted her nose.

Mama Terry reached the bottom of the stairs with an evil scowl on her face. Over on the bed was proof of her suspicions; the bolted chain was all the evidence she needed. She knew her son was doing the devil's work. So, she decided she would teach him a lesson.

She quietly walked over to the bed with her paddle in hand. She whacked him hard as she could. "Back you damn devil!" She yelled out.

"I say get thee behind me, Satan!" She was in a fit of rage.

Over and over, she swung the paddle. Raining down blows of pain upon the tiny figure huddled in the bed.

28

"Back! Back! I tell you! Get behind me, Satan!" She continued wailing away.

The first blow brought Lolo out of his medication induced slumber. He bolted straight up.

Some old woman was beating the holy shit out of him.

He tried his best to shrink away from the old lady but with the collar shackle on it was futile, but that didn't stop him for trying. He jumped off the bed! On the bed, off the bed, and so forth.

All to no avail. Even though he ate the two plates of food. He had gone too long without food. Lolo was suffering from malnutrition. His physical weakness got the best of him. Finally, he just laid on the bed curled up in a ball and hoped the old lady would tire out soon.

"Back, Satan! You and your filthy spawn!" She kept chanting as she repeatedly hit him.

Just when Lolo thought he could not take any more, the beating stopped.

"I will not tolerate demons or devils under my roof! I'll beat the heathen out of you if it's the last thing I do! You little Dirt Bag! You need church!" Without another word, Mama Terry stormed out of the basement.

Lolo stayed in the fetal position terrified wondering what the fuck just happened and who the fuck that was beating the holy crap out of him!

Now he knew that there were at least two mentally deranged people in the house. The logical question would be just how many people were there in total?

His body was beyond sore. She might have been an old lady, but she was a strong old lady. Clearly, she was senile, judging by her ranting and raving. One of them religious fanatics that believed the entire world were sinners except for them.

They were God's chosen.

CHAPTER FOUR

School had let out over an hour ago. Lolo wanted to wait an additional hour, but his growling stomach and hunger pains wouldn't let him. He figured enough time had gone by, so it was time to make a move. Last week some kids from school were hanging out at McDonalds clowning around after school so he wanted to let enough time pass to make sure they wouldn't be around.

The McDonalds dumpster was always a jackpot around that time of day. He was lucky again; he found a bag with twelve uneaten sandwiches in it. The workers would toss burgers that had sat for too long in the dumpster as they did that day.

Lolo was so hungry he tore into one of the sandwiches before he even stood up. When he did stand up it was with a mouth full of McDouble with cheese. The overstuffed bag in one hand, McDouble in the other with the biggest grin he could fit on his little face.

That was until he saw them, the kids from school were back. "Eww... what are you doing in the garbage can?" one girl asked.

"Look he's eating the garbage!" another pointed out.

"Eww! Gross!" They all began pointing and laughing at him. "Garbage Boy! Garbage Boy!" They taunted him until one of the bigger boys walked up to him. "Sniff, sniff."

"You even smell like garbage. And look how dirty his clothes are..."

"He's been wearing that all week." Another boy cut him off. "And his T-shirt says Dirt Bag!" One of the girls pointed out.

"He is a dirt bag. Aren't you, Dirt Bag?" A fat kid started chanting, Dirt Bag over and over. Soon they all joined in calling him Dirt Bag. He couldn't do nothing but cry. It wasn't his fault he didn't want to be a dirt bag, but he didn't have anybody to care for him or love him. He was all alone. He dropped the bag of food and the burger in his hand, climbed out of the dumpster and ran away crying.

The next day, Lolo was starving since he didn't get to finish eating the day before. He looked around, there was one car at the drive thru, but it left. He didn't see any of the kids lurking outside, so Lolo made his way to the back of the parking lot. He was determined not to let what happened yesterday happen again.

Once he got back there, he jogged over to the dumpster. He braced himself to climb into the dumpster.

Just when he touched it, he heard.

"Hey, Dirt Bag!" When he turned around to see who it was that caught him. It was Stephanie.

Stephanie was the girl that first asked why he was in the garbage yesterday.

"Are you about to go dumpster diving again? You don't have to do that, here." She reached inside of the bag that was in her hand and removed a Big Mac. She held it out in front of her like she was offering him the burger.

"Here, do you want it?" she asked with an innocent look.

Lolo didn't know what to say. He was so embarrassed to have gotten caught again. Plus, he was hungry, but he didn't know if he could trust her.

"It's okay, I won't tell anyone. You want it don't you?" This time he slowly nodded his head up and down.

"Then come get it. Come on." He walked over to her. When he reached her, she turned and threw the sandwich. "Then go fetch it, Dirt Bag!" she yelled.

Then added, "Here's some fries to go with it." She turned the bag upside down and dumped the French fries on the pavement.

"Eat it boy! Come on, Dirt Bag. Eat it boy!" The rest of the kids had been hiding behind the dumpster. They all came *out and teased him instantly, calling him names and laughing at him.*

It wasn't his fault that his mother died. Thinking of his mother and how unfair God was for taking her from him. He quickly became agitated. Before he realized what, he was doing, Lolo hauled off and punched Stephanie right in her big, fat mouth.

He busted her lip. This time it was her time to cry. All the rest of the kids just stared at the two of them in shock. He bent down grabbing a handful of fries and shoving them into his mouth. Next, he ran off laughing.

**** N. D. ****

Lolo made his way to the bed and sat wondering, if God was truly real, where was He at? Why did He allow so much fucked up shit to happen him? Why did everybody who ever loved him die? Lolo wanted answers. He just wanted to know the reasoning behind it all.

His stomach began bubbling bad. A sharp cramp shot through his side that made him grab his stomach and double over, wincing while he did so. His body wasn't used to the richness of the food, and this was the result. Not to mention running and jumping all over the bed trying to escape the crazy lady with the paddle, no doubt had everything all shook up.

Lolo accepted the fact that he wasn't about to be able to hold this back. So, he forced his aching body up to go handle his business. When he stood up, he realized his real problem, the only thing he had to use the bathroom in was the urine basin. There was no way he would be able to squat over that little thing and be successful in aiming what was inside of him into the little pan.

Desperation was etched upon his face as he sought out another source. He really had to go now! He was about to say forget it and go right there on the floor and then he noticed a darkened painter's bucket. Another cramp shot through him. The cramp subsided and he went for the bucket. Once he reached it, he didn't waste any time plopping straight down and letting loose.

He sat on the bucket for a full ten minutes. He realized that he left the toilet paper that someone placed on the TV stand while he was sleeping. Lolo didn't want to get up without wiping himself, but if he didn't get up, he couldn't get the toilet paper. What a dilemma he found himself in. On second thought he remembered the guy was a creep, there was no telling what the kidnapper had in mind.

Lolo decided he should do everything in his power to get filthy. Maybe if he got too nasty the pervert wouldn't want him. Lolo thought that was sound logic. Following that logic, he decided to get up from the bucket and climb back into the bed without wiping himself clean.

**** N. D. ****

The succulent aromas floating in the air was working Terrence's saliva glands overtime. His mouth was so watery he had to swallow every ten seconds or so to keep from salivating on himself. He closed the oven after inspecting the roast. Dinner should be done in another thirty to thirty-five minutes. Tonight, he was making a succulent roast with carrots and red potatoes baking in the pan with it. Garlic butter mashed potatoes, steamed asparagus, and a salad on the side. Delicious indeed.

Since he had some time to kill, he walked upstairs. There were four bedrooms upstairs. His mother's room was at the end of the hall on the right.

Purposely for privacy, Terrence moved from his original room, which was next to her room. Now he was in the room across the hall from his original room. The house was built back in 1954. It was a solid house, but an old house. The bedroom walls and doors were so hollow he could hear her fart in her room while he was in his. Those weren't the sounds that made him change rooms. It was her extracurricular activities. Every night she would play gospel talk radio loudly while she watched porn on the TV and fornicated with herself. It was sickening to hear her, and it drove him crazy.

When he was younger, Terrence spent several years studying carpentry in school. He used those skills to make changes around the house. Soundproofing the basement was first. Next came the steel reinforced doors on both the basement and his room. He had to keep the old bitch out of his business.

Mama Terry was a sneaky, nosy motherfucker, always spying and eavesdropping. He fixed her though. Only he had the key to his room and the basement. He walked down the hall to her door, stopped and listened. Just like he thought. He could hear some old preacher delivering a soul snatching sermon. Satisfied, he walked to his door and unlocked it. Inside he took a moment to admire the room. It was set up perfectly.

A California king size bed was positioned in the center of the back wall. Across from the bed were two flat screens TV's. One was hooked up to cable, and both were connected via Bluetooth to the monitors he had for the security cameras.

Above the bed mounted to the ceiling were two more flat screens. All four monitors were 55-inches. Hidden cameras were positioned in places strategically, to observe the entire house. Next to the bed was a custom stand he built for his creams, lotions, and toys.

Terrence sat on the bed and picked up the remote to turn on the two TV's in front of the bed. Out of habit, he checked all the cameras inside and outside of the house. Satisfied that nothing was out of place he laid back so he could see the ceiling and turned those monitors on with the same universal remote. When they came to life, the screen on the right was the camera in Mama Terry's room. She was laying on top of her comforter, spread eagle masturbating. On the screen in her room a porno movie was playing. His mother was the biggest hypocrite Terrence ever knew. All the self-righteous, love Jesus bullshit she forced onto people. Yet every night she watched Byron Long's big cock, fucking one porn star after the other.

35

The screen on the right played the feed from the camera installed inside of the basement. The camera itself was the newest HD 360 high resolution camera with its 360-panorama viewer, Terrence was able to see the entire basement.

Lolo was laying on the soiled sheets of the bed in the fetal position, sleeping. During his tossing and turning because of the nightmare he was having; the filthy blanket had been knocked off him.

He laid there helplessly unaware of the sadistically perverted eyes that lustfully stared at his naked body. In just the short time that he's been held hostage, Lolo has put on some much-needed weight. His ribcage that was once completely visible was now barely showing in some places. His little arms had grown as well as the chicken legs he was walking on the night of the torrential storm. He put on weight, but they were not the areas that Terrence was focusing on.

Like the perverted fuck that he is Terrence's eyes lustfully roamed over every inch of Lolo's naked behind. Slowly, in desperation, he allowed his eyes to drink in every single detail. He hadn't noticed that his breathing had become labored. He was panting like an animal. Looking at Lolo, Terrence began thinking of the things that he wanted to do to such young, sweet, innocent flesh.

Deep inside of his heart, Terrence knew what he was doing was wrong. But he could not help himself. He knew what he was doing was sick and perverse. Yet, he couldn't stop himself. In his mind it wasn't his fault that he was a sick, twisted fuck. They made him this way; they created the monster that he was.

When Terrence was younger, he found himself in the same position as Lolo. Terrence was once the young innocent victim, locked away in a dark room, made to do unspeakable sexual acts for his mother and her Bible toting pastor and boyfriend. Not only did they molest poor little Terrence, but they also tortured and beat him as well. Pastor Young called it spiritual cleansing and atonement. In truth, Donnell Young, aka Pastor Young, was just a sick low life pedophile who used the insecurities of women like Mama Terry as a means to carry out his despicable and disgusting fantasies.

The pastor and Mama Terry performed every sexual act imaginable on young Terrence. Even doing things so sick that the average mind couldn't even conjure imaging such things. Terrence's issues began with him role playing some of the same things Pastor Young did to him with some of the other little boys in the neighborhood. Until one little boy did the same to his little sister. When the boy's parents caught him, he told them it was a game that he and Terrence played. Once the parents confronted Mama Terry who did nothing about it. The police were called, and word got out.

Young Terrence was ostracized and labeled as a weirdo and a fruitcake. It got so bad that he was forced out of public school. Which meant he would be homeschooled. As it turned out, perverted ass Pastor Young readily volunteered to teach him. That's when young Terrence was introduced to his own form of Hell on Earth!

As Terrence's level of arousal heightened, he began to touch himself. In his mind he was Pastor Young, and Lolo was him. The longer he stared at the screen, the more aroused he got. Then his eyes moved to the other screen. The one with Mama Terry masturbating. The sight was now gloriously appealing to his sick mind. He began jacking off, looking at her. In his mind Terrence was fucking his mother like she used to make him do when he was old enough to maintain an erection. It never failed; history was doomed to repeat itself. Every time he thought of what she did to him, anger and hate replaced arousal.

Why did she turn him into a creep?

He was her darling little Terminator. That is what she used to call him in order to cheer him up. Whenever he was sad, she always told him that she loved her little Terminator. Especially when she wanted him to go down there and taste her little "Sweet Tart."

"Come on Terrence be Mama's little Terminator. Don't you want to be my little Terminator? Then lick Mama's Sweet Tart for her, Terminator."

"Aaaaaargh!" Before he could snap out of his trance, Terrence threw the remote control against the far wall. It crashed between the two flat screens so hard it shattered into thousands of pieces.

"You fucking bitch! You old fucking lizard pussy, bitch!" He bolted from his bed yelling as he stormed towards her room. His now flaccid penis bobbed in the air. He didn't even bother tucking it back into his pants. "I fucking hate you, bitch! Do you hear me? I fucking hate you!" He began banging on the bedroom door with his fist.

"Devil child!" Mama Terry shouted, "For in you lies demons in the thousands. You are surely the spawn of the Dark One who dwells in the bowels of the earth, waiting for his release! I rebuke you, Satan! Get thee behind me!"

"You bitch! You are Satan! I'll fucking kill you bitch!" Terrence was literally on the verge of going berserk.

"No weapon formed against me shall ever prosper! Not even you the Son of Satan!"

"I'm going to kill you, bitch!" With murderous thoughts on his mind and evil of the highest degree harbored in his heart Terrence stormed to the kitchen to grab a large knife.

"It's your fault you cunt bitch! I'll show you who's evil. I'll show you cunt bitch!" he mumbled all sorts of vile stuff to himself as he marched.

As Terrence got closer to the kitchen the mouth-watering aromas returned. Taking his mind off killing his mother and reminding himself of his duties. He still needed to feed the boy. He had already spent too many hours planning and working on getting the little boy ready.

CHAPTER FIVE

No Mom. You're my mom." A tearful Lolo cried bitterly. "I don't want another mom."

His little brain could not take what he was being told. "Thomas, listen to me honey. I will always be your mama. I love you, Thomas, and that will never change." She kissed his tears away while she held her little baby. "But you need to know the truth Baby, Mama doesn't know how much time she has left. And you need to know your true legacy Baby. You need to know that you do have family out there who will love you just as much as I do…"

"No, Mama! No!" Lil Thomas cut her off again. His poor little head was shaking from side to side, desperately trying to free his mind from what he just heard.

For six and a half years Jennifer had been the only parent that little Thomas Smith Jr. had ever known. She was his entire world, and he was her everything. Then she got sick. She was eventually diagnosed with Stage II breast cancer.

First, she tried radiation and chemotherapy sessions, but to no avail.

When she had no other options, a mastectomy was performed. Unfortunately, not even that helped. Jennifer was dying. She figured before she died, the nephew that she had raised as her own child should know the truth. The entire story.

So, she began telling him, he was the son of a once feared and respected leader of a drug cartel. His father, Thomas Smith Sr. or T'Rida as he was known in the streets, was the leader of the notorious Neva Die Dragon Gang. He had been killed in a shoot-out with the police long before little Lolo was born.

T'Rida was married to his childhood sweetheart, Monique. They had two children, Titas and Na'Shay. Anne was his mistress.

His mother, Anne, or Chiba as she would later come to be known as, was a revered and feared member of the She-Wolves. A sisterhood of assassins tied to the Neva Die Organization.

Anne was killed at the hands of her little brother Sutton, whom she had raised since their parents' death. Sutton was the leader of a gang of hyenas called Young Nigga Mafia who decided to take Neva Die to war. Challenging for the supremacy of the Bay Area's underworld.

Jennifer didn't want to share this information with Lolo. Yet she knew it was important for him to know. As Jennifer held Lolo in her arms, she silently prayed that God would take his pain away. One person shouldn't have to experience so much loss.

As the tears rolled down her cheek Jennifer pleaded with God in her heart to give her more time. Not for herself, but so she could be there for her baby.

Gently she just rocked him in her arms telling him that everything would be okay. Over and over, she assured him. Her words became more convicting, and the rocking became violent shaking.

Repeatedly, violent shaking. It wasn't a dream.

It was real!

"Lolo wake up." He heard Mama Jennifer telling him.

Instantly Lolo opened his eyes. He was back in the basement, still trapped. Terrence was standing over him, shaking him, and attempting to wake him up.

"Get off me! Don't touch me!" Lolo demanded as he quickly sat up.

"I brought you some food." was all Terrence said. For a long minute there was awkward silence.

Neither spoke. Both were lost in their own thoughts. Finally, Lolo built up the courage to speak.

"What do you want from me? Why am I here?" he asked in a voice that was devoid of any emotion.

However, emotions swam through Terrence's head. He hadn't expected the onslaught.

"I-I helped you." Terrence began. "You were out in the cold, wet, and hungry. So, I helped you." His voice was innocent, almost childlike.

"Help me?" Lolo was confused. "If you want to help me, then why am I chained here? Why can't I leave?" his voice wavered as he asked the last part.

Terrence leaned in closer to Lolo, and he. held his breath and braced himself for whatever.

"Sssh! It's because of her. I am protecting you from her.

She's mean. I have to protect you." Terrence's voice was full of sincerity as was the look on his face.

"I don't wanna stay here. I wanna go! Let me go." Lolo whined.

"No!" Terrence snapped. Instantly his body language and demeanor changed like Dr. Jekyll and Mr. Hyde just that quick, his concerned look was replaced with a hideous evil scowl.

"No, shut up! You can't leave! It's not safe. Here, eat your food!" He picked up the plate of food and held it out for Lolo.

"No! I WANNA LEAVE!" Lolo screamed.

With lightning quick speed, Terrence slapped him across the face. Hard.

"You can't leave. It's not safe. Now, shut up and eat!" Terrence was furious now.

"But…"

Terrence slapped him two more times.

"Eat the fucking food you little Dirt Bag!" Those were exact words Mama Terry said to him when she beat him with the paddle those weeks back.

Lolo sat there with a blank expression on his face. Terrence was about to slap him again but stopped in mid-swing.

A puzzled look came across his face. Then he stood up straight as a board, turned on his heel and walked away.

"Ungrateful little Dirt Bag!" he mumbled to himself as he left.

When Terrence walked out, Lolo was left alone with nothing but his memories and his thoughts. Now that his Mama was gone all he was left with was his thoughts and memories. Finally, he picked up the plate of cold food. No matter the outcome. No matter what his fate might be. He would need his strength and energy for whatever came next. Thus, he had to eat.

As he ate, he began thinking more about the things Jennifer told him. But instead of looking at them as memories, Lolo was beginning to see that they were lessons. She was preparing him for the world. Preparing him for muthafuckas like these. The sick, twisted, evil, and foul muthafuck'n predators that were in the world.

The world is full of predators and prey, victims, and victors and Lolo refused to be a victim. Terrence would pay dearly for everything that he did to Lolo. This he vowed as he rubbed the place on his face where the blows landed.

Yeah, Terrence would surely pay! Again, he allowed his mind to drift.

**** N. D. ****

When you get older Lolo, (Jennifer had started calling him Lolo due to his low profile, demeanor, and his low persona when he spoke). You are going to hear lots of stories about your father from a lot of different people. Not everything that you are going to hear will be positive, because not everyone liked your father. But honey your father was a great man, and no matter what anyone says about him, everyone who knew him had to admit he was a man of integrity and morals… do you know what those things are?"

Lolo shook his head, no… he had never heard either word before. "Integrity is when a person takes ownership and responsibility for their actions. And morals are the things that define a person's right or wrong logic. A man will always take responsibility for anything he does. And he will stand up for what he believes in.

"That's how your father was Baby. He stood for what he believed in, and he accepted the consequences for his actions. Never let someone make you do anything you don't wanna do. Even if that person is bigger and stronger than you. One day you will become bigger and stronger than them." Jennifer's words and teachings would soon come to help him gather the strength needed to endure.

Lolo eventually dozed off because of the sleeping medication that Terrence was putting in the food before serving it to him. Brining him vivid dreams of the only mother he'd ever known. Except this time, he also thought about the mother he didn't know.

He thought about Anne.

**** *N. D.* ****

"Okay, class. That was the bell, class is over, and school is out. Before you leave, make sure you turn in your class assignment." Mrs. Dickerson walked over to her desk and began grading some papers.

Lolo loved school. He loved learning new things and hearing about faraway places he could not imagine. Every day he dreaded going back to where he was staying. He thought about running away, but he didn't have the slightest clue as to where he could go. He did know one thing without a doubt, and that was he hated where he lived.

When Mama Jennifer finally passed, her brother Robert reluctantly took him in. Robert was an alcoholic who loved to drink. The issue was he became violent when he was drunk. The real problem was he drank every day to the point of violent drunkenness, and he took it out on Lolo.

He reluctantly left Mrs. Dickerson's class and roamed around the neighborhood, lost in his thoughts. There was no doubt in Lolo's mind that Robert would already be drunk by the time he made it to the house. So, he decided to take the long way home to prolong the inevitable beating that was to come once he stepped over the threshold of his house.

Sure, Robert would be upset that he took longer to get there. The way Lolo saw it, he was going to get beat no matter what, so why worry about doing the right thing?

It took him twenty minutes to reach to reach the park, which he inevitably cut through to avoid his classmates who liked to hang out at one of the boys' house that just happened to be on the way to Robert's house. The day was a beautiful one. The temperature was in the high 70's with a slight breeze. Who would've figured that such a day would bring his classmates to hang at the park instead of Dontae's house?

By the time he noticed them it was too late. They had already saw him. There was enough distance between them and him that he could've turned around and walk the other way.

The problem with that was, that he would look like a coward.

Mama Jennifer always told him, "Never pick a fight and never run from one. If people think you are a coward, they will constantly pick on you. Stand up to a bully, Lolo and he will back down. Back down from a bully and he will always bother you."

He never broke his stride. He just continued moving forward. Beads of sweat began to form on his forehead as his nerves became alert.

"Hey, Dirt Bag. Where are you going?" Dontae hollered; he was the worst of the bunch.

Lolo kept his head and eyes straight and kept walking. "Yeah, where you are going, loser?"

"When was the last time you bathed, you look dirty?"

"Look how nappy and dirty his hair is. Eww, he's a nappy headed tar baby, Dirt Bag." They'd all surrounded him by now as they hurled insults at him like sticks and stones.

"Why'd you hit my girl last week, punk?" Stephanie was Dontae's girl.

Again, Lolo didn't respond. However, he could no longer keep walking because Dontae was in his face.

"Yeah, Punk! Why'd you hit my sister, you sissy?" That was Fat Pooh. He was Dontae's best friend and flunky.

"Look...I don't want any problems." Finally, he spoke. "Ooooooh... he don't want problems." One of the kids teased.

"Well, you got problems now, punk." Another kid proclaimed.

Someone popped Lolo in the back of the head. He could tell they weren't going to stop messing with him. They had their minds set on teaching him a lesson.

His palms become sweaty as his heart began pumping faster. The fear factor was present, but he would not allow it to become evident.

"You wanna know why I did it? Huh?" Lolo lowered his head, balled up his fist and looked Dontae square in the eyes.

"Because she kept fucking with me. I don't like people fucking with me and your bitch of a girlfriend was." His comment not only wasn't expected, but it caught all of them off guard.

"What you…" The question never finished coming out of Dontae's mouth.

Lolo socked him square on the jaw. He didn't stop. He continued raining blow after blow, down on Dontae's face.

Being the coward that he was, Fat Pooh snaked Lolo from behind. Once Pooh jumped on him all of the kids jumped in. So many fists were coming from so many directions, he couldn't do anything about it.

While the pack all jumped Lolo, Dontae recovered. He picked up a large rock and cracked Lolo in the head with it. His little body dropped like Tommy Gunn when Mike Tyson knocked him out.

Once he hit the ground, they all started kicking and stomping him, while calling him Dirt Bag repeatedly.

Shoes landed against his head, arms, chest, and legs. Someone kicked him in his groin, and he howled in pain. Poor Lolo had never felt an anguish like that before. The pain was short lived when someone suddenly kicked him square in the eye. This not only made his eye swell, but it also knocked him out as well.

His sore and beaten body lay helpless in the park on such a lovely spring day. All the kids thought he was dead because he had stopped moving. As is the nature of children, they all got scared and ran away.

When Lolo finally woke up, he was badly battered. His entire body was sore and one of his eyes was swollen shut. He didn't let any of that bother him though. Lolo stood up and began walking to Robert's house with an upbeat spirit and a smile on his face. In his head he kept replaying the picture of the blows he'd delivered to Dontae. He was sure that he wouldn't be the only one bruised at school tomorrow.

CHAPTER SIX

Oh, when the saints, go marching in. Oh, when the saints go marching in.... Oh Lord, I want to be in that number. Oh, when the saints go marching in." Mama Terry sang her church hymn as she sat at her workstation sewing.

Her mind may have been on Jesus, but her heart was most definitely in league with the devil. She was a confused woman who grew up abused and battered. It began with her stepfather raping her when she was only nine years old. Only to start a cycle of neglect, molestation and abuse that would span over thirty years. Abusive behavior trickled down to her own son when he eventually was being abused by her.

Her mother used to tell her that she had the spirit of Jezebel in her. Though no one could say if that was true or not, one thing was clear to all who knew her. Something evil lurked in the heart of Mama Terry!

"That's it! That should do it." She cheerfully told herself.

It had been a mighty long time since she'd had someone to sew for. The motor on the sewing machine hummed as she put the final stitch in.

Once she finished, she held her work up in front of her face for inspection.

"And the Lord sewed fig leaves together to make for them garments, which concealed their nakedness." Mumbling a verse out of the book of Genesis to herself as she snipped the thread free of the machine.

She stood up and made her way to the basement. Slowly she unlocked the door and descended the steps while humming, "Oh when the saints come marching in."

The air in the basement was musty and stale. At the bottom of the landing, it was noticeably hotter by a few degrees.

51

Lolo sat Indian style on the bed staring up at the large old woman that came in and beat him for no reason the other day, with a look of concern on his face.

"Hello there, Baby." He didn't respond to the ugly old lady.

Instead, he looked at her like she was crazy. All sorts of thoughts ran through his head as he stared blankly at her. "Hi, are you still mad at me for the other day? I'm so sorry, Baby. Sometimes, Mama Terry just gets a little carried away when I'm doing the Lord's Will. Yes, I do. Yes, I do now. Look, Mama made you something so's you wouldn't be mad no more." She brought her arms from behind her back holding a pair of underwear she'd had just finished making for him.

"See, don't these look nice? I made them especially for you because you are a beautiful looking little man." At age ten there was no way, shape, form, or fashion he could resemble a man. Not even a young man at that.

"Don't be rude. Answer me."

When he still didn't budge or make a peep, she began to get angry at him. Mama Terry quickly crossed the distance between them.

"I said here, Goddamn it." She thrust them in his face.

"I don't want nothing from you." He defiantly told her.

Mama Terry smacked the living shit out of poor little Lolo.

She hit him so hard his ears were ringing. "I said take them, you lil' Dirt Bag."

"No, bitch! I don't want them!" Mama Terry recoiled from his words like he'd slapped her in the face.

The blood in Mama Terry's veins boiled. She couldn't believe the little shit had the nerve to call her something so vulgar.

"Why you little motha…." She bit her bottom lip and stomped up the stairs.

Once she reached the kitchen, she was fuming. "And I will strike my wrath down upon thee and vengeance shall be mine said the Lord Their God!"

She didn't have a clue what she was looking for, but she knew that God would show her the way. When her eyes landed on the stove, she saw the small pot of water that she was boiling for tea but had forgotten about it. It had been boiling for so long that most of it had evaporated.

There was only about a cup full left in the steaming pot. Thinking it was God talking to her, telling her what to do, she snatched the pot up in a jerking motion that almost made her scold herself. She was oblivious to this. Mama Terry was on a one-track mission, cleansing the little Dirt Bag. As she was coming down the stairs, Lolo became very alarmed at the sight of the pot with steam rising from it.

"No! No! No! Wait!" He began his desperate plea, but his voice and words fell on deaf ears.

Lolo jumped up from the bed. "Lady, wait… I'm sorry! Please, don't do this Please I'm sorry!" she ignored his cries and pleas.

With the neck shackle there wasn't anything he could do. Nowhere he could go to escape.

His little heart thumped rapidly in his chest! His eyes bulged large and for the second time in his life Lolo pissed on himself.

Mama Terry took one look at the stream of hot urine sprouting from his penis and was appalled. "Little nasty, filthy, disrespectful, Dirt Bag!" She flung the water at him.

"AAAAaaaarrgh!" The scream was piercing.

Lolo's body jerked and twitched. The scalding water instantly melted away the skin it touched.

"I baptize you with the Lord's Holy Water, you Dirt Bag" After this Mama Terry left the basement feeling good about herself.

Meanwhile all Lolo could do was lay still, so as not to disturb the sensitive blisters that begun forming on the places that water touched and didn't peel the skin off. The pain was excruciating to say the least. Not one tear escaped his eyes. He held them in, refusing to allow either of the two weird muthafuckas the satisfaction of seeing him cry ever again.

Fuck no! He was thinking about Mama Jennifer all night and this morning, his real mother Anne, and his biological father, T'Rida.

How would they feel if they saw him now? Shaking and cowering down like a little baby? What would they say? They would be ashamed that's what!

They wouldn't want to see him like this. He had to fight back. Lolo knew he had to start plotting his way out of here. No matter what he had to do or how, he knew one thing for sure. He would make them pay severely for all that they've done!

With a fire in his eyes and a blaze in his heart, Lolo fought through the pain and began doing pushups. He needed to ignore the pain. Needed to be able to turn his feelings off through sheer will-power. Most importantly he needed to be stronger.

From now on he would channel the hurt. He would use the pain as motivation. Since everyone wanted to call him and treat him like a dirt bag. He would show them a dirt bag!

He would no longer be low key and mild mannered. He realized the world was dog eat dog. Lolo was dead. Once he gained his freedom, he would only answer to Dirt Bag! Dirt for short!

**** N. D. ****

Terrence knew something was wrong. He could feel it in his bones, but he didn't know what it was. He stared intently at the screen, yet he just couldn't figure it out and it was messing with his mind. Finally, he decided to go and get a better look. All the while he was making his way to the basement Terrence could not shake the feeling that whatever was wrong Mama Terry had something to do with it. The meddling bitch was always snooping around. Putting her nose in places it didn't belong and messing things up.

One look was all it took. The boy was badly burned all over his body. There were boils all over the place. In some places there was no skin. A clear milky liquid coated the open areas.

The look in the kid's eyes was different. It was a look that Terrence was intimately familiar with himself. It was the look of pure, unadulterated hatred. He knew it because it was the same look that plagued his eyes.

Terrence's heart sank deep in his chest. Only he knew what the boy was feeling right now, because he'd felt it himself a long time ago.

"What, you've come to do something too." It was more of a statement than a question.

"I-I. No. Who did this to you? How did it happen?"

These questions weren't aimed at the boy. Terrence was pondering things out loud.

"Don't act like you don't know your mother did this?" Dirt's voice was flat.

"That cunt bitch! I told you I was trying to protect you. She's evil!"

"And you're not?" the question surprised and hurt Terrence. "W-What? No-no! I'm not evil! I'm the good one." His feelings were genuinely hurt, and his voice again sounded like a small child.

56

"They're the bad ones, not me. I'm good." He lowered his voice before adding, "They hurt me too. It's okay I'll help you though this. But you gotta be quiet and promise to be good."

"What?"

"You have to behave if you want me to help you."

"Okay." Lolo did not understand what was going on, but he'd go along and find out where he was headed.

"What's your name?"

"Dirt. What's yours," he replied.

"What kind of name is Dirt? The stranger asked.

"It's my name." Dirt told him flat out.

"Okay Dirt, I'm Terrence. But they call me Terminator." He stood up "I'll be back. I'm going to help you, Dirt." Then he left. Ten minutes later he was back with a first aid kit, a bottle of aloe vera and his hands covered with a pair of latex exam gloves. He sat everything down on the nightstand. Then he looked at Dirt.

"Remember be good." he warned Dirt.

Lil Terrence pulled a set of keys out of his pocket and motioned for Dirt to come closer. When he did Terrence reached and unlocked the shackles.

"Thank you." Dirt really meant this.

"I told you I'm gonna help you."

Over the next thirty minutes lil Terrence helped Dirt dress his wounds. The two of them spent the entire time talking like they were the best of friends.

Dirt felt good inside because he knew this was working in his favor. He didn't quite know how, but his gut told him it was.

Lil Terrence was just happy that Dirt was talking to him. The other times he was down in the basement Dirt wouldn't speak to him.

When they were finished dressing the wounds, lil Terrence said he had to go it was almost dinner time. He was so excited he left and forgot to lock the shackle back around Dirt's neck.

As soon as the door closed Dirt jumped into action. He didn't know if he would ever get another opportunity like this again. He had to take advantage of it. The first thing he did was find a way to put the shackle back on without locking it. Once he accomplished that task, he became frantic. He was in search of a weapon, anything that could help him escape.

The first place he searched was the old woodworking station. As silently as possible he opened every single drawer. Drawer after drawer he opened with no luck. His poor little heart thumped louder than the African Humdrum. All he had on was the underwear that Mama Terry made for him. However, he began sweating. Inside the second to last drawer, he found an old, rusted carpenter's screwdriver. Dirt hurried up and snatched it out of the drawer. It was one of those real thick, flathead screwdrivers. About twelve inches long and an inch and a half thick, with a nice heft to it.

Dirt's heart swelled as he began to get excited. The screwdriver would most definitely come in handy, yes it would. He needed somewhere in the dark basement to hide it. No matter where he looked, nowhere seemed good enough. Finally, he decided to stash it under the right side of the mattress.

Even with the screwdriver, Dirt knew he still had his work cut out for him. Terrence was a mountain of man. Besides there was two of them. Deep in his heart he didn't know if he could do it. But he knew he didn't have a choice. He had to try and save his life because he was on his own.

Dirt could hear voices upstairs. It sounded like people were arguing. Slowly he crept up the stairs, paying close attention to the voices. As he neared the top of the stairs, he stopped with four steps remaining. His heart pounded away inside of his chest. He didn't dare think of the consequences he would face if he got caught. He could make out Terrence and Mama Terry's voices. The two of them were having an intense argument about something. Silently he claimed another step. The lock on the door was old-style you needed a key to unlock from both sides. The keyhole was about the size of a nickel.

Dirt held his breath and brought his eye to the keyhole. He was able to see most of the kitchen and a portion of the living room. Something was cooking on the stove, and it smelled delicious. He mentally checked himself.

Now was definitely not the time to think about food.

"How many times must I tell you that the Lord knows all, and he sees every little wicked thing you do, boy?" He couldn't see Mama Terry because the wall separating the kitchen from the living room was blocking her. But he knew her voice.

"What about you, huh? You dirty, cunt bitch! Does the Good Lord see all of your little secrets? Huh? Does He see your sins?" Terrence's side profile was two thirds of the way visible along with a third of the back of his head.

"You watch your vile he-bitch mouth in the Lord's house, you heathen!" Mama Terry shouted.

"Tell me, Mother, how would you like it if I threw a pot of boiling hot water on you?" The question must've frightened Mama Terry because the tone and sound of her voice changed.

"Terrence, you wouldn't do that to Mommy would you? My lil' Terminator wouldn't hurt Mama, now would he?" Her voice was pleading. The fear made her voice tremble.

"Then you better stay away from him, you fucking-cunt bitch! He's my friend and I won't let you hurt him!" Terrence banged on the wall when he said this. His voice was threatening, revealing his anger.

"I promise, Baby I won't hurt your little friend again. I'm truly sorry." Mama Terry's voice sounded as if she was on the verge of tears.

Dirt was all confused, he didn't know what to make of her behavior. One minute she was evil and strict. The next she was nice and sweet, pleading like a little girl. It was as if she was two completely different people.

Terrence told her to go to her room while he served dinner. He would bring her food to her. Dirt took that as his cue to go back down the stairs.

CHAPTER SEVEN

Ten minutes later, Dirt heard the basement door open. Terrence was coming downstairs with his meal.

Terrence smiled before saying, "I hope you like it. It's homemade lasagna."

"Will you eat with me?" Dirt asked. A funny look came over Terrence's face. "Please, I'm lonely. Plus, I'm still frightened." Dirt added for emphasis.

Terrence thought for a minute, and then smiled.

"Okay, let me get my plate." Terrence was so happy he couldn't conceal his excitement.

While he was gone, Dirt debated whether or not, he should make his move. Finally, he decided if the moment presented itself, he would take it. If not, he wouldn't try anything. He didn't want to rush and mess things up. Right now, he had the advantage. He would use this opportunity to make his abductor think they were becoming friends.

No sooner did he make his mind up, Terrence came back down the stairs. He had his plate in one hand, a cup in the other, and a big smile on his face. He shuffled his way to the bed and sat down. The two of them sat together eating and watching the Big Bang Theory on the TV. They laughed, joked, and talked for over thirty minutes. If a stranger overheard them, they would swear two kids were eating while having a sleep-over. Terrence behaved and talked like a little boy.

Dirt fell asleep ten minutes after he took his last bite.

**** N. D. ****

His entire body felt like it had been run over by a Mac Truck. He laid in bed all night last night and all day today.

He skipped school, not because he wanted to, but because he honestly couldn't move a muscle. After getting jumped in the park yesterday, he didn't make it back to Robert's until after 7 p.m.

First Robert talked shit for almost an hour about him getting the shit beat out of him. Then he proceeded to do the same thing and beat Lolo's ass even more.

Lolo couldn't take it any longer, he had enough of the abuse. Enough was enough! Sometime in the wee hours of the night he made his decision to run away.

As bad as he wanted to leave last night, his body just wouldn't let him. Tonight, he didn't care. He would manage to get through the pain.

His opportunity came a little after ten o'clock, once again, Robert drank until he passed out. The pain he experienced just to move was excruciating, but Lolo managed to get the fuck up out of the house.

It was a house of horror from the beginning. The beatings caused him to live in constant fear every day.

When he wasn't getting beat, he lived in fear wondering when the next beating was coming. And when it finally came, he was in fear that Robert would kill him.

He laid there in the abandoned, rundown house wishing he would have planned his great escape a little better.

He hadn't had the opportunity to eat anything. Now he was starving like a runaway slave.

He missed Mama Jennifer so much. When she was alive, she always took care of him. Mama Jennifer would know what he needed well before he did. With that warm smile of hers, she was the perfect mother.

His thoughts were interrupted by the sounds of someone coming into the house. Earlier he had found a nice thick stick while he was walking. He kept thinking it would make a nice weapon, in case someone bothered him.

Lolo wrapped his little hand around the stick, squeezing it for security. In his condition he wouldn't be able to do much. But goddamn it! He would try! His heartbeat sped up in anticipation.

His worries were put at ease once he saw who it was entering the abandoned house.

The house was a single story three-bedroom house. A few of the windows were broken out. And the back door hung on one hinge for everything it was worth.

There was trash all over the place. But other than that, it was in fairly good shape. There were no feces anywhere and the water was still on.

He lay very still. As still as he could while keeping his eyes pinned on her. It was the hooker that came in with a guy earlier and had sex with him. Lolo couldn't help but watch the entire thing. They were only about fifteen feet away from him but never knew he was there.

She walked to the bathroom. He still had a good view of her from his hiding spot. The bathroom door was off which gave him a very clear view inside of the bathroom.

She lit a small candle and then got undressed. Lolo was wondering what she was up to. Everything made perfect sense when he saw her take a hand towel and soap dish out of the big purse-like bag she was carrying.

Lolo watched in awe as she bathed in the sink. It was the first time he had ever seen a female naked. He knew he should give her some respect and privacy, but he could not take his eyes off of her. She was beautiful. Her body had curves which appealed to him.

While watching her clean herself the candle served grave justice in illuminating her body. Lolo noticed two things that he couldn't see in the dark of the house.

First, she was young herself. She looked to be about fourteen or fifteen. The second thing that he noticed about her was that she was fucking beautiful.

She was about 5'2". Her skin was a real light yellow, almost white. She had the body of a seventeen-year-old, not a fourteen-year-old. Her eyes were big like a doe, set in a face that looked like she'd been kissed by an angel.

His heart began racing. He felt like the air around him had gotten thinner making it hard to even breathe. For some reason, his mouth had gotten dry, and he couldn't swallow either.

For a full fifteen minutes he watched her bathe herself in a hypnotic trance. When she finished cleaning herself, she reached in her bag and pulled out a fire red thong and slowly stepped into it.

He received the shock of his life when she turned around and said, "I was wondering if you were gonna be here when I came back." He froze like a deer in headlights not knowing what he should do.

He wanted to run, thinking he was in trouble for spying on her. He didn't utter a word.

"Oh, okay so you're a shy one huh?" she asked him with an arched eyebrow. "Well, you weren't so shy while you were standing there watching me wash my coochie" She didn't sound angry or seem upset. So, he took his chance.

"I-I'm s-sorry. I shouldn't have done that." He spoke barely above a whisper.

"It's okay, honey," she assured him with a smile on her face. "Did you like what you saw?"

"Y-you're beautiful!" This got a chuckle out of her. She sounded just as lovely as she looks. He was ashamed of how he stared at her during her private moments.

"Come on now. I promise I won't bite. I might gobble you up, but I won't bite you." She giggled.

He worked up his nerve and slowly shuffled to the bathroom where she was. The closer he got, the faster his heart raced.

Finally, he was within arm's reach of her. She was flawlessly beautiful up close.

"Oh my God! What happened to you?" The level of concern in her voice made his eyes water.

When he was able to trust his own voice, he looked dead in her eyes. "Life." Was all he could say.

Out of pure instinct she took him into her arms. "Ouch!" He winced. "Oh, I'm sorry honey!" She immediately released him.

"Where does it hurt?" she asked him.

"You smell good," was his only response. This brought a good laugh out of her.

She asked him again, where was he hurt. Instead of answering her, Dirt took off his shirt. This time it was her eyes that watered. She took him into her arms again.

This time the embrace was soft and gentle.

Her tears fell and triggered something deep inside of him and for the first time since Jennifer's death, he cried.

The two of them stood there under the candlelight, just holding one another. Silently crying in each other's embrace.

Finally, she released him. Then grabbed the candle and her bag and led him into the back bedroom. It still had a real bed inside of it. The bed had new sheets and blankets on its full-size mattress.

"What's your name, honey?" she asked him once they were both sitting on the bed.

"Thomas Smith Jr. But my mama called me Lolo." His head was leaning on her mature breast, so his voice was muffled.

"Lolo, I'm Nyomi. Who did this to you?" Her voice massaged his pain away.

Right there in her arms Lolo told her everything. When he finished a massive weight was lifted off his shoulders. Afterwards the two of them laid down, with him in her arms. It was the best sleep he'd gotten since Jennifer died.

After that night, the two of them grew really close to each other. She was the only good thing he found in a world full of shit. They had spent countless hours talking and dreaming about the future.

She made him laugh effortlessly with her bigger than life dreams. Nyomi told Dirt that she would become a huge star and he believed her. To him she had enough sunshine inside of her to light up the entire room.

She told him that she was just turning tricks to survive on the streets, but also so she could save enough money to go to Hollywood one day to fulfill her dreams.

**** N. D. ****

Looking around the basement, Dirt's good mood was slowly fading away. He needed to get free from the basement and find Nyomi. She was all he had, and she needed him.

He climbed off the bed, he needed to relieve his bladder.

That's when the straw broke the camel's back, and his good morning was ruined. Anger began building. How could he have been so careless and stupid? Last night Terrence refastened the shackle around his neck and locked it.

The need to take a piss vanished as he sat back down and mentally kicked himself in the ass for making the foolish and costly mistake. Before he lost all hope, he climbed over to the other side of the bed and checked under the mattress for the screwdriver. He let out a deep sigh of relief when he felt it. All wasn't lost. He just had to make a mental note to pay closer attention to what he was doing.

Still, he felt optimistic about him escaping this hellhole.

Dirt got off the bed and pissed in the chamber pot. Taking a seat back on the bed after handling his business. He laid back and thought about some of the times he and Nyomi had.

**** N. D. ****

Lolo hated when Nyomi left to sell herself. He'd heard enough stories from Mama Jennifer about the streets, and he'd seen enough to know that the world was a cruel place. And within this cruel place were a lot of evil people.

He sat in the abandoned house worried for Nyomi. He hoped she would return soon.

The idea of having money was great. He had to admit the perks it allowed them, like not having to eat out of the dumpster for one or being able to buy soap and other toiletries. He had no idea how many simple things he took for granted until he was out on the streets.

Things like toothpaste, soap, toilet paper, or something so simple as where you were going to lay your head that night. Finding Nyomi was the only good thing that had happened to him since Jennifer died. Just when his worrying increased, she came in through the back door. Since Lolo was staying with her, Nyomi decided that she wouldn't bring any more men to the house. She did not want Lolo to be anywhere near when she did what she did.

"It's about time you showed up. I was getting worried." Relief was written all over his face.

"I'm sorry, honey. I stopped and picked up a few things that we needed." Lolo saw the two bags in her hands, but he was feeling some kind of way. At that moment he was still in his feelings, so he asked.

"Nyomi, what am I supposed to do if one day you don't come back?" Nyomi heard the fear and sadness in his voice.

"Aww... honey, come here." She met him halfway and took him into her arms.

"I will always come back. You know why?" He didn't have a clue, so he shook his head no as tears fell from his eyes. Everybody always left him.

"Because you're my little boyfriend." she told him with a bright smile.

This got his attention fast! Lolo stopped the flow of tears and looked her in the eyes.

"I am?" Was all he could manage to get out.

"Yep. Sure, you are. And I got something for you too." To his reluctance she let him go and walked over to the bags. She reached into one and retrieved a Jack in The Box bag. When Lolo saw the bag, he lit up. But he had to play it cool, after all he was her man now. He couldn't be no cry baby punk! Playing it off as cool as he could, he grabbed the bag and said thanks.

"Where's yours?" he asked her.

Nyomi pulled out another bag and together they ate their food and talked. When they were finished, Nyomi got up to take a bath. She only took a bath every two days. With the house being abandoned, she didn't want to draw suspicion from the water department. If the water department found out water was being used in an abandoned house, they would send someone out immediately and shut the water off.

Lolo figured since he was her man now, he needed to help pull his own weight. Since he couldn't make money, he decided he would be as helpful as possible.

With his new position in mind, Dirt got up and headed for the bathroom. He was going to wash his woman's back and take care of her.

When he turned the corner, the candlelight cast funny shadows on the walls. There was a strange smell in the air. A sweet pungent odor. He noticed that it got stronger the closer he got to the bathroom. He entered the bathroom and saw that the glow wasn't coming from the candle, but directly from a lighter's flame. Nyomi was lighting something that she held in her mouth, while soaking in the tub.

When she noticed he was standing there she simply just kept inhaling. Lolo waited for to finish before he asked her, "What's that?"

"It's medicine, honey." she told him before placing the glass stem back to her lips and taking another hit.

This time she closed her eyes, leaned all the way back in the tub and tilted her head backwards before releasing a column of sweet, pungent smoke in the air. When she opened her eyes, they were full of lust.

"Is something wrong, honey?" she asked him in a sultry voice. "Huh? No..." Lolo was too busy gawking at her large breasts that were sticking out of the water since she was leaned back in the tub. "I-I came in so that I could wash your back for you."

"Ooh... that's so sweet and its gonna feel sooo good. Do you want some of the medicine?" she asked, extending her hand with the crack pipe in it towards him.

"Okay." He couldn't be a chicken now that he was her man.

She put the pipe to his lips and lit it. Lolo sucked on it like he saw her do. When he couldn't pull no more, he swallowed it, held it for a few seconds like she did and then blew it out.

Immediately he felt weird in a good way. His heart rate sped up, his mind started racing a mile a minute and his entire body was tingling.

Nyomi smiled up at him remembering her first hit. "Come on, honey. You can wash my back another time. Right now, I need you to do something else." Nyomi got out the tub.

Nyomi led him by the hand to the back room. He'd never had an erection before now. But as he followed her young firm ass cheeks as she walked, his little man was giving her a standing ovation. Once they got in the room, they both sat side by side on the bed.

"Lolo, do you want me to be happy?" Ny asked in the sexiest voice while batting her eyelashes at him.

Lolo was too choked up. He had a bullfrog the size of Texas lodged in his throat. So instead of speaking he nodded his head.

"Do you want me to make you feel good?"

71

"Y-yes." he stuttered, but at least this time he spoke.

He didn't know if he was feeling the way he was because she was butt naked in front of him, or if it was the medicine.

"Will you do something for me?" She placed another rock on the pipe as she laid out on her back. "Eat my coochie for me, honey." Nyomi was so horny her little pussy was volcanically hot, and she needed it doused.

"H-how?" He would do anything to make her happy. "I'll show you, honey. Put your mouth down on it."

Nyomi lit the crack pipe and took a huge hit. She held it in until she almost passed out. Slowly she released the smoke and coached Lolo on how to eat pussy.

CHAPTER EIGHT

Lolo woke up with Nyomi in his arms feeling like a new person. Granted he did not actually sleep with her. He followed her coochie eating instructions well enough to give her three orgasms.

He climbed out of the bed and went to go take a piss. As he relieved himself, he thought about how he could make some money as well so Nyomi could be happy. He settled on breaking into houses. As small as he was no one would think twice if they saw him approaching a house. After washing his hands, he ignored his growling stomach and headed back to the room.

When he walked in, she was sitting up in bed. The sheets and blanket were down exposing her large, firm breasts.

Again, Lolo felt his private getting hard.

"You want me to eat your coochie again?" he asked eager to please her.

Nyomi couldn't speak because she was holding in the smoke. Instead, she gestured for him to get closer. When he did, she pulled his erection out. He didn't know being big was a good thing, so he was embarrassed.

First, she started blowing smoke on it and then took him in her mouth. She began sucking on him while the rest of the smoke escaped around her lips.

Poor little Lolo didn't know what to do. Being a prostitute, Nyomi was far more advanced sexually than he was. She was going to teach him some new things today. Lolo just closed his eyes and enjoyed it. What she was doing to him was the best thing he'd ever felt in his life.

Nyomi paused for a minute to pick the pipe up. "After I take my hit, you take one. That will make this feel even better." She did and then he did, and she was right.

His dick got even harder when she blew the smoke on it again and continued sucking it. She didn't expect Lolo to be as big as he was. He had to be at least 6-7 inches. This turned her on. While she was giving him an expert blow job her little fingers were teasing her hungry coochie. Selling her body to survive had turned her into a nympho and sucking on his seven-inch dick was making her hornier and hornier by the second. Finally, she couldn't take it any longer. Nyomi had Lolo lie on his back. He had to bite his bottom lip as she slid down over his dick. Lolo hadn't even ever seen a porno movie before. He was so frightened; he didn't know what to do.

As Nyomi began slowly sliding up and down on top of him, being clueless was no longer a problem.

He reached out and grabbed ahold of Nyomi's hips as his natural male instincts took over. Each time she slid down on top of him, Lolo would thrust his inexperienced hips toward her trying to feel as deep inside her warm, safe channel as he could go. He raised up and took one of her breasts in his mouth. He didn't know why he did this, it just felt right. Nyomi arched her young back and grabbed one of her breasts. The moment she pinched her nipples her movements became more animated. Taking his signs from her, Lolo freed one hand and covered her other breast.

"Ooh... yesss Baby." Nyomi tilted her head backwards in pure, pleasurable bliss.

Instead of squeezing one nipple, Lolo pinched one and lightly bit the other. This caused Nyomi to get wild. So, he pinched again, this time pulling slightly on them as he did so.

"Oh! Fuck! Yes, lil' Daddy! Lolo, smack my ass, lil Daddy. Smack it!" He quickly did as she asked.

"Ooh lil' Daddy! Do it harder." "Harder!" Again, he did.

"Lil' Daddy Fuck me!" By now he was thrusting upward just as hard and fast as she was.

Faster and faster, harder, and harder.

"Ugh huh! Ugh huh! Spank me lil' Daddy! Make me cum!" She screamed as her movements were at a rapid pace.

He didn't know what she meant by make her cum, but he knew he had a funny feeling at the base of his stomach.

His testicles became tight.

He did like she instructed and started spanking her hard. Only not with one hand. He was spanking both of her ass cheeks. He would spank one and then the other.

"Yes! Yes! Do it lil Daddy! Ooh fuck! Ooh fuck! Yes! Yes! Here it comes! Yes! Yes! Oh fuck!

The way she screamed and collapsed on top of Lolo scared him. But that something that took over him wouldn't allow him to stop pumping.

He grabbed and squeezed both of her firm ass cheeks. This appeared to bring Nyomi to life. She tried as best she could to fuck back but her orgasm did her in.

Instead, she put her lips to his ear and talked that shit. "Come on lil Daddy, fuck this pussy. Ooh Baby let me know that I'm making you feel good and claim this pussy, honey claim it! Fuck me hard, lil' Daddy. fuck me!" That did the trick.

Lolo shook and convulsed like a seizure patient as he had his very first orgasm. After jerking and shaking for four full minutes, he finally collapsed too. He was out of breath and definitely out of energy.

"W-what was that?" he asked when he finally regained his breath.

"That's sex, silly." She smiled at him.

Jennifer had spent every waking moment trying to teach Lolo everything she knew with the time she had left. She had covered as many topics as she could think of. However, the birds and the bees weren't one of them.

76

He'd never heard of sex, and when he told her so, Nyomi couldn't believe her ears. She finally got up enough energy to roll to the other side. Her bare breast was pressing up against his arm.

"Did you like it?" she asked quietly looking into his eyes. With a huge smile on his face, he posed his answer in the form of a question.

"Can we do it again?" This brought a peal of laughter from Nyomi.

The feeling of her nipple sliding back and forth over his arm caused him to get excited again. When Nyomi saw his new erection, she knew he was serious. She decided to show him how serious she was. Nyomi decided she wasn't going to go to work that day. They laid up in bed having sex over and over. Nothing good lasts forever though, which was the soundtrack of Lolo's life.

Later that evening, Nyomi got her period. Considering she was not due for another four days she had not gotten her tampons yet. Wanting to take care of her in his new role as her boyfriend Lolo told her he would run to the store and get them as well as grabbing something for them to eat. Nyomi gave him thirty dollars. She was grateful to have him go to the store for her. It would have been hell if she had to go herself. The cramps she was feeling had her doubled over in pain. Finally, she balled up in the fetal position once he left, trying to lessen the cramps.

Ever since George Speedy's Supermarket and Head's Liquors closed, the only store in East Menlo Park was the Amigo store CrossRoads Market, on Willow Road. Lolo went there first and then decided he was going to take the alleyway to Jack in the Box.

The night was beautiful. Clear skies full of stars and a slight breeze.

Lolo's mind was stuck on sex. He wasn't paying attention to his surroundings. In fact, he didn't have a care in the world. The cool night air made him feel more alive.

The back door of the taco spot opened. Lolo always kept to the shadows. Therefore, Armando, the owner of the shop never saw Lolo.

77

"Look everything you asked for is in the bag. It will be on the passenger seat of my car. Yes. Yes. I will leave the doors unlocked. No worries, no one comes back here like that. Just give me five minutes then come get it. Okay." Armando hung up the phone as he made his way to a Buick that was parked in the shadows.

He looked around before removing a black bag out of his coat and tossed it inside the car. Then he made his way back to the kitchen of the taco shack.

Once the door was closed, Lolo ran over to the Buick. Sticking to the shadows he didn't waste any time. The way he figured it, something important was in that bag. Why else would the guy be acting all secretive?

Lolo opened the door, reached in, grabbed the bag, and got the hell out of there as fast as possible. He made it three blocks to Jack in the Box in a few minutes. After placing his order, he went to the bathroom and locked himself in the bathroom stall. Lately it seemed like his little heart was racing all the time. However, it was excitement that was causing it this time.

When Lolo opened the bag, he knew right away his suspicions were correct. He quickly closed the bag and exited the restroom after placing the black bag inside of the grocery bag that contained the tampons. When Lolo returned to the counter, his food order was ready. Eager to get back to Nyomi to show her what he found, Lolo snatched the food and bolted out the door.

It took him five minutes flat to run from Jack in the Box back to 1300 block of Sevier Avenue, the location of the abandoned house three and a half blocks away.

He was so excited to be able to be contributing to the team that he didn't hear the muffled cries until he was a couple feet from the bedroom door. It could've been Nyomi crying from the pains of the cramps. Yet something told him that wasn't the case. He stopped dead in his tracks.

Cautiously he peeked his head around the corner. What he saw made his heart weep. Rage filled his veins. Someone was on top of Nyomi raping her. Her cries were muffled because the filthy muthafucka had one of his hands covering her mouth silencing her, but Lolo could hear her cries. He panicked at first, he thought he didn't know what to do. It was his fault that this was happening because he had left her alone. Defenseless.

While he stood there trapped inside his own personal purgatory, Nyomi turned her head facing him. Their eyes locked. Her eyes pleaded for him to help somehow. Upon seeing the fear and hurt in Nyomi's eyes, a single tear escaped his eye. Suddenly he had the answer. In a trance like state, he retrieved the black bag out of the grocery bag.

When Lolo unzipped the bag and reached inside of it, he came out with a snub nose .38 special. All black with a rubber grip. He'd seen it when he opened the bag in the restroom.

"Hey! You bitch ass nigga!" At the sound of his voice, the muthafucka stopped in mid stroke and turned his head around.

Even in the dim light Lolo could tell it was the John she had brought back the day they first met.

His ugly, scarred face was covered in sweat. When he first turned his ugly head, he had a scowl on his face.

Angry at being interrupted, his face was blood red. It wasn't until his eyes landed on the .38 special in Lolo's hands that the look went from anger to shock and fear. "W-w-whoa man! Whoa! Let's just take it easy now.

Everything is okay. It's not what you think." The bitch ass nigga reeked of fear and Lolo could smell it.

"Get yo bitch ass off of her!" The command sounded almost like a growl; it was so menacing.

"O-O-Okay, okay. Just wait a minute now." The would-be rapist was scrambling to get himself together.

79

He fumbled for his now limp dick trying desperately to tuck it back inside the soiled boxers.

The rapist was in such a hurry to comply that he stumbled over his pants that were pulled all the way down to his ankles and fell face first.

While he was scrambling, trying to get himself in order. Nyomi jumped off the bed. Her lower body was covered in blood. As were the sheets that she was laying on. The sight caused a new rage to soar through Lolo's body.

"O-okay now look, I'm s-sorry okay? W-why d-don't you t-tell me how I can make this right, okay?" The sorry son-of-a-bitch was stuttering over every word.

Desperately trying to fasten his now pulled up pants. "There's no reason f-for any b-body t-to get hurt, now i-is there?

The shame, hurt, and betrayal that Nyomi felt from being brutally violated sent her mind to a dark place. As she stood up pain shot through her vagina, proof that it wasn't a dream. Looking at her attacker, all she could think of was revenge.

Lolo ignored the pervert. He glanced towards Nyomi and said, "I'm so sorry, Baby." He meant it from the bottom of his heart. "What you want me to do?"

"Give me the gun." Her voice sounded like Angela Bassett when she played in "Waiting to Exhale." "I gotcha Ny. Just say the word and I'll do it."

"Give me the gun!" Lolo desperately wanted to defend her, but he realized he couldn't understand her pain or her state of mind.

He felt he couldn't defy her or deny her this.

"Look inside the bag." He told her without taking his eyes or the gun off the rapist.

"W-wait a m-minute now! Let's talk about this…" his cries fell on deaf ears just as Nyomi's cries had done.

The look on her face once she found what was in there was somewhere between a sinister smirk and a devilish grin. In her hands was the chrome version of the pistol gripped in Lolo's hands.

"H-Hold, hold up now! I got money. Surely you kids could use some money. I-I can g-get you an apartment and t-take you away f-from this filth!" he pleaded with his hands up in a placating gesture.

Nyomi stepped towards him. "Let's talk about it! We can talk!"

She walked directly up to him placed the barrel of the gun on his crotch and pulled the trigger!

His screams were music to her murderous ears. The rapist cried a symphony as he collapsed right on the dirty floor.

Ny fired again. She felt invigorated His screams were almost orgasmic to her ears. The slug tore into his stomach, sending him yowling in pain again.

Lolo didn't want to rob her of her revenge. But he didn't want her having the weight of committing murder on her young shoulders, it was his job to protect her.

He walked straight up to the rapist who was crying like a bitch on the floor.

"Look at me." When he didn't get a response "Look at me muthafucka!" Lolo shouted.

When he looked at Lolo, his eyes were filled with pain and terror.

Lolo's were filled with righteous fire as they stared back.

Lolo emptied every single bullet into his head. This was the first time he caught a body. Lord knows it wasn't the last.

Nyomi stepped up so that she was standing side by side with Lolo. First, she kissed him on the cheek. "Forever, lil Daddy. I'm yours. Forever."

Then she pointed the chrome executioner at the lifeless body and emptied her gun into him.

CHAPTER NINE

Dirt could feel himself getting stronger. It had been almost three months since Terrence first kidnapped him and put the shackles on his neck. In the beginning the shackles rubbed the skin around his neck to the point of chaffing. But now the skin was tougher, like Dirt was.

He'd begun working out after the second week. He started off doing ten sets of five which was fifty pushups. Now he was up to a thousand. Five hundred in the morning and five hundred at night, twenty sets of twenty-five.

Mama Terry constantly harassed him. Every couple of days he could count on her whooping his ass. Most times she would beat him with either an extension cord, switch, or coat hanger.

The skin where she'd splashed the boiling water on him left some ugly scars. Reminders for him to analyze every choice before making them. Not doing this was how he'd ended up here in the first placed.

Some good points have managed to make their way through. His eyes had adjusted so well to the dark that he'd developed some sort of night vision. He could see almost completely in the pitch dark.

Also, Terrence had become very social towards him. He came down the steps and ate dinner almost every night with Dirt. The entire time the two talked and joked like they were best friends. Dirt knew that he was weakening the defenses and security that Terrence once had set up within himself.

More and more times he allowed Dirt to remove the shackle from around his neck so he could move around freely. Dirt rationalized this could only be so because Terrence had a way of monitoring him. This caused him to believe there was a camera or cameras set up somewhere in the basement.

Believing that to be true, Dirt never touched the screwdriver that he'd found a couple of months back.

The best news yet was his body's response to the sleeping pills or whatever Terrence had been putting in the food. Over the three months that he'd been taking them, Dirt's body has begun to develop some type of resistance or tolerance to them.

It started with Dirt not staying asleep for nearly as long as he was in the beginning. As time progressed, he stopped getting sleepy period.

Knowing that this would be to his advantage, he has been faking like he's falling asleep. So far, it's been almost two weeks since he began faking it and Terrence hadn't caught on to him yet.

He was going to make his move soon.

**** N. D. ****

The two young killers had no choice but to leave their abandoned home since that they were in Menlo Park and chances were slim that none of the neighbors called the police to report the shooting. However, there was no way for sure to tell if "Shot Spot" picked up the shots or not.

Nyomi learned about Shot Spot when one of her clients was running it down to one of his lil homies on the phone. With it, the police could pinpoint with accuracy the location of any gunshots occurring in the city limits.

They didn't have any place to go. The afternoon had quickly turned to night, making it both unsafe and unwise for them to be out on the street. Especially with what was in the black bag.

Nyomi knew there was dope in the packages. Along with the guns and dope, there was also money and a folder containing photos and information on a middle age Hispanic woman.

The package that Lolo intercepted was in fact, a contract on Armando's wife, along with the payment for the hit. In total there was five thousand dollars and two kilos of pure cocaine. The .38 specials were supposed to be the weapons used in the attack.

Armando's wife had been sleeping with his best friend, Hector. Hector mysteriously drove his car off a cliff in Santa Cruz due to brake failure.

Esmeralda would not be so lucky for her disrespect; Armando wanted her death to be done in the open and he wanted it messy.

This way he would send a message to all his so-called friends and his enemies, that Don Armando Ruiz Riviera would not be made a fool of.

No plan is foolproof, Lolo's interception of the package was proof of that.

Nyomi decided to call the only person she thought she could remotely trust. She called Von Jack. Von was one of her weekly clients. He always seemed to worry about her safety and well-being, plus he always paid her more than her fee.

Another reason she turned to Von was that he was the one that supplied her with the crack to get high. He sold dope in the Gardens which is a hood in East Palo Alto. Von was always bragging to Nyomi about how much dope he sold, and all the money he had. She knew if anybody could help them, it was Von. So, she made the call.

Von picked the two of them up and drove them to a rundown, roach infested motel in Redwood City, called the Capri Motel. It was a motel that inmates with nowhere to go once released from the County Jail were sent to by the Service League, calling it a shit bag was a compliment.

Upon their release the Service League would give the homeless inmate a voucher that they could take to the motel in exchange for a room.

Pulling up to it, they saw all types of shady characters and lowlifes. The motel itself looked like something out of one of those old black and white horror movies, the ones with the vacancy sign ready to fall.

Von parked and went to get the room. While he was gone Lolo reminded Nyomi not to tell him anything about what had happened or about what they had.

When Lolo first laid eyes on Von something about him didn't sit right. Listening to what Lolo told her, Nyomi simply told Von that she got her period so she couldn't work. She promised him a freebie for his help, once her period was over. The low life muthafucka didn't ask any questions, he simply jumped at the opportunity.

A dope fiend who looked like he hadn't showered in a month sneakily approached the car.

"Hey there little ones, what y'all got going on?" He had the look of a weasel and the eyes of a slithering snake.

87

"Nigga, get yo muthafuck'n ass away from my shit!"
Von barked when he came out of the office.

The dope fiend slithered away like the slimy snake he was.

Once he climbed back into the car, Von handed the room key to Lolo, who he believed was Nyomi's little brother. He drove to the back and parked in front of room 9, the same number that was on the room key.

"You guys want me to come in with you and stay for a little while so these muthafuckas around here won't know y'all by yourselves?" Von's stare alone was intimidating.

At 6'2, 276 lbs. he was very intimidating on the outside. Those who knew him though knew that his intimidating statue was completely misleading. Inside he was a marshmallow.

"Naw, we good big Homie." Lolo spoke up before opening the passenger door and getting out.

"Thanks, Von. We really do appreciate you doing this for us. I'mma call you as soon as Aunt Flo passes, I promise." Nyomi turned and looked towards him. "No problem, lil' mama. Can a nigga at least get a kiss before you go?" He licked his lips with a lustful look in his eyes.

"Not in front of my little brother, Babe. I told him that you were a friend of our father's." she lied smoothly.

Nyomi just wasn't going to disrespect Lolo by kissing another nigga in front of him, regardless of the circumstance or relationship.

Von didn't give a fuck about her little, punk ass brother, but he would respect her wishes. After all, he was looking forward to his freebie plus Nyomi had given him $600 to pay for the room for a week. The clerk only wanted $285.

Not only did Von get a free date out of the deal, but he also kept the $315. So, there was a smile on his face knowing that he scammed her.

When Lolo opened the door, the smell was the first thing to hit them. It reeked of stale cigarette and drug smoke, sweat and cheap sex, a lot of it.

Inside the room there was a raggedy wood chair, a rinky-dink twin-size bed that looked like the owner dug it out of a dumpster, and a wooden nightstand that was going to collapse at any moment.

Lolo walked in first, stepping on a carpet that had too many stains on it to count. The stench was even more assaultive to their nose.

"I know you're tired Ny, but don't touch anything. I'll be right back." There was no way in hell Lolo was going to allow her to sleep in the sheets on that bed.

"Where you going?" she asked, feeling nervous.

"To get you something better to sleep on." This brought a smile to Nyomi's face.

Lolo opened the door then paused, "Lock the door behind me, I have the key so don't open it no matter what."

"Okay." As soon as the door closed Nyomi did as he told her. She smiled because it felt good to have someone care.

She walked to the bathroom thinking that she would run some bath water. One look at the stained bathtub changed her mind. Finally, she tried the chair then sat in it waiting for Lolo to return.

Outside Lolo was just reaching the office. The brotha working behind the counter looked worse than the dope fiend that walked up to Von's car.

"What you need, lil Homie?" The clerk eyed him with very little interest.

"Say uh…" Lolo reached into his pocket, "I bet you $200 that you got at least one room in this place nice enough that you'd sleep in, and $200 that you got some brand-new sheets and blankets back there." Lolo counted four bills out of the roll of money that was in the black bag.

Seeing the money in Lolo's hand got the nigga's full attention. His full undivided attention. Looking at the money, he licked his lips like the wolf in that old Little Red Riding Hood cartoon.

"It's just for the two of you?" The clerk asked with the wheels in his scheming mind turning.

"Just until my brother comes back," Lolo tried his best to sound convincing.

"Okay I'll tell you what," he reached under the counter and came back with another room key. "Why don't you guys take room 11, that should take care of that. And let me grab you some fresh sheets and a new blanket." He scurried off to go retrieve the stuff.

He was back in less than a minute later with an armload of sheets, a comforter and a couple of pillows, all still wrapped in plastic. "Here you go. Now is there anything else I can help you with?"

The greed was written all over his face.

"Nope, this is good right here." When Lolo reached for the bundle of stuff, the chrome .38 special slipped off his hip. The clerk's eyes got as big as two donut holes.

He picked it up and stuck it in his waistband. Lolo reached inside of his pocket for another Benjamin Franklin.

"As a matter of fact, you ain't seen nothing." He handed the clerk the bill.

"I don't know what you are talking, bout, lil Homie." He grabbed the money and put it in his pocket.

Lolo made it to the door then he called over his shoulder, "Bet you another two you can't find me a box of bullets."

"I'll call you when I get 'em."

Nyomi was so happy five minutes later when they were sitting on a queen size bed with new sheets and a new comforter, inside of a clean room. Lolo relaxed on the bed, lost deep his thoughts while Nyomi went inside the bathroom to shower and get herself together.

Lolo had to figure out their next move. They couldn't stay at the Capri forever. Hell, from the way things looked around there, Lolo didn't want to stay at the motel long anyway.

Nyomi was all he had. They were two lost souls trapped in Hell's mirage of life. His age no longer played a factor. Neither did the fact that Mama Jennifer died before she could complete his crash course on life. All that mattered was they had each other to depend on.

His thoughts were interrupted by a rapping knock on the door. Turns out the clerk was able to find a box of bullets for him. After paying the man, Lolo loaded both guns. Then he went to check on Nyomi.

He heard his baby crying when he got close to the door. When he opened the door, she was sitting up with her arms wrapped around her bent legs. At that moment she looked vulnerable, crying like the sweet little girl she was. The reality of what happened to her had finally hit her.

Lolo couldn't imagine what to stay to a person in such a state as this. He simply kicked his shoes off and climbed inside the tub with her. He sat down behind her and held her in his arms. Not caring about the clothes, he had on or anything he just held her and rocked her gently letting her know that it was okay.

92

CHAPTER TEN

Alone tear escaped Dirt's eye as he reflected back on that day. Even now, he could still feel her pain and sense the shame and embarrassment she must've felt at that moment.

How badly he wished he could turn back the hands of time. If he could, if it were possible, he would go back before leaving to go to the store that night, he would stay and protect her. All so he could take her pain away.

Dirt realized it was that exact moment, holding Nyomi in the bathtub of that cheap motel that he actually fell in love with her.

He couldn't allow himself to be sad or get down. Now was the time when he needed to channel everything and use it as motivation.

He got up and began his exercise regimen using his hurt and pain as motivation. He had to get out of his current predicament. Every day that he spent downstairs trapped in that dungeon are days that could've been used finding his baby! Five months of working out and eating the good, healthy food that Terrence cooked had put 40 lbs. of muscle on his "5'6" frame. He no longer looked like the skinny, malnourished looking Lolo. He damn sure didn't look like a ten-year-old boy.

With no mirror down in the basement with him, Dirt couldn't see the transformation of his body, he could however feel the change in his strength.

Terrence on the other hand saw full well the difference in Dirt's physique. He also noticed a new level of confidence that Dirt hadn't possessed in the beginning. There was a difference in his posture and demeanor as he worked out and walked around the basement.

Terrence watched the workout routine so much that he knew when Dirt was nearing the end of it. He got up to retrieve the wash bucket and take it to Dirt along with a couple of towels.

Making his way to the basement all sorts of evil homosexual, pedophile thoughts played in his mind as they did every time he watched the little boy. Terrence would catch himself watching Dirt and fantasizing about his young, firm body. It sickened him that he often had fantasies of doing to the boy the same horrible sordid things that Pastor Young did to him.

The times when he would catch himself doing such filthy things, he would punish himself the way Pastor Young would punish him with the belt of fire.

The belt of fire was an old 1 ½ inch police belt with metal rings where the holes should be. That wasn't its main component though. The belt had been dipped in crazy glue and then dipped in crushed bottle glass. Each time it struck Terrence's flesh as a kid the results were disastrous. The glass would bite into his skin like angry viper fangs, tearing and ripping the skin. It was the worst pain a child could ever experience physically.

Now Terrence welcomed the bite of the belt of fire. Its sting he felt cleansed his soul of all his transgressions.

He descended the basement steps to find Dirt drenched in sweat. Breathing deep and slow like a male lion. Even in the dark of the basement the sweat made his skin shine.

"How many did you do?" Terrence asked already knowing the answer.

He'd counted every single rep as he spied on Dirt from inside his room.

"Six hundred." Dirt didn't like when Terrence asked him about his workouts.

To Lolo it felt like he was keeping track because he had something planned.

"You're getting stronger and stronger every day, that's good.

Dinner will be ready in about forty-five minutes." Terrence turned to leave until Dirt called him..

"Do you think we could eat upstairs tonight? I promise I'll behave." He knew the answer would be no. It was always no.

Feeling guilty for his earlier thoughts, Terrence decided he would allow Dirt a few minutes up top.

"Sure, why not. But don't try anything, or I'll promise you'll regret it." If Dirt thought, he was going to pull a fast one. Terrence was more than ready to teach him a lesson.

"I wouldn't dare try anything T. We're buddies ain't we?" Another trick Dirt was using to weaken his defenses or guard was giving him the nickname "T". Dirt hoped it would make Terrence feel a little more personal.

Terrence didn't answer him, he simply gave Dirt a puzzled look and then left. Dirt grabbed the face towel and soap and began washing up. Everything was coming together. Little by little he would gain more and more of Terrence's trust until he found the opportune time to strike and gain the upper hand.

After washing Dirt sat back on the bed watching Power on Starz network until dinner was ready. Terrence hooked the cable up for Dirt once Dirt had gone a month without causing any trouble.

Dirt liked Power. He liked Tommy more than he did Ghost, he could relate to Tommy more. Ghost had a strong mind and Dirt studied how he used it. The way he thought through situations. Just as Tasha fixed Tommy a plate of food on the screen, Terrence returned to tell Dirt that dinner was ready.

Dirt walked up the stairs in front of Terrence. He told himself to take in every single detail and store it in his memory which he did.

The kitchen was the standardized kitchen inside houses in the hood. The tile counter and cabinets lined one wall. The next wall housed an old, stained stove with a beat up looking yellowish refrigerator next to it. Dirt noticed that all the countertops were bare

95

except for the pans of food. There was not a knife or utensil in sight. To the left was a small wooden circular table with four chairs around it. Dirt headed in that direction until Terrence instructed him to turn right, in the direction he witnessed Terrence arguing with Mama Terry a little while ago. As Dirt passed the wall that was blocking his vision back then he noticed two things; first, to the left was the living room. Again, it was your standard living room equipped with a couch, love seat, flat screen TV, and a cabinet. The second thing that caught young Dirt off guard, to the right, the way Terrence had been facing that day arguing with Mama Terry, there was only a wall there. A very large antique mirror hung on that wall. It was a very beautiful piece of work. It had a gold hand crafted frame around it, that had sculptures of angels and cherubim carved and sculpted into the gold. Dirt doubted if he could fit in the space in front of the wall. So how did Mama Terry?

"Open that door there and wash your hands and face. You must wash thoroughly before you sit down at the table." He pointed to the door directly in front of Dirt.

Dirt followed the instructions and opened the door. It was a bathroom. A new face towel was folded on the sink next to a bar of Dove soap with Shea Butter. "Use that face towel there." Terrence pointed out before heading back to the kitchen to tend to the food.

The bathroom was spotless. One could tell that someone paid close attention to the tidiness of it. He picked up the soap and smelled it. The Shea Butter smelled so good. He relished the smell. The only thing Terrence had brought to him before this to wash up was a bar of cheap Ivory soap.

Dirt didn't have a problem taking his time ensuring that he washed thoroughly. Between the feeling of hot water on his skin and the scent of the Shea Butter, he almost didn't want to leave the bathroom. After cleaning up behind himself, Dirt opened the bathroom door and paused. Right there less than twenty feet away from him was the front door.

He looked towards the kitchen to see what Terrence was doing. Dirt didn't see him. In his heart Dirt believed he could make it to the front door before Terrence ever suspected anything was wrong.

He licked his lips as he weighed his options. Freedom was right there. Just a mere fifteen to twenty feet and the torment was over!

"Hold up." he actually heard the small voice in his head warning him. It was too easy. Ghost wouldn't go for something that simple. It had to be a trap.

"Sure, why not? But don't try nothing or I'll promise you'll regret it." He played Terrence's threat over in his head.

This had to be a test. Fucking door probably needed a key to open it.

Dirt smirked. He wasn't going for none of the bullshit. Just like Ghost told Tommy, "I ain't going for the okey-dokey."

"I'm surprised you didn't try to go for the door. Actually, I thought you were going to try it." Terrence spoke when Dirt walked back into the dining room and sat down.

"Why would I do that? I told you, we're friends now." Dirt was glad he'd made the right choice.

He sat down at the table and waited for Terrence to bring the food. This time the meal consisted of roasted lamb with a garlic basil sauce, wild rice and vegetables, and a glass of Sherman Oaks Red Wine.

"Where's Mama Terry?" he asked Terrence once he sat down at the table.

"She eats in her room." Terrence answered.

Dirt thought that was a little odd, especially since he didn't see, nor hear anything.

Then again, they were both weirdos to begin with. The two of them sat and ate in silence.

CHAPTER ELEVEN

The first night inside the Capri Motel Lolo stayed awake all night. He lay with Nyomi in his arms and the all-black .38 by his side.

Ny needed a good night's sleep to escape the nightmares of real life. She needed her rest, but Lolo needed to be alert. The motel was that shady.

Staying awake was good for him. It gave him all those hours of silence to analyze the severity of their situation.

They were two kids alone in the world with two guns, a few thousand dollars, and a bunch of dope. That was way more than anybody needed to make something happen. To get on their feet or to make a way out of their situation. However, that shit wouldn't last long so he needed to come up with a game plan. Laying there, he did just that.

When Nyomi finally woke up he went over his game plan with her. Silently she was impressed with how he was stepping up to the plate when he was needed.

As much as he hated to leave her alone, they both knew that they were going to need supplies because Lolo had decided they would stay at the motel for a couple of weeks. This would give Nyomi time to rest and heal from the physical scars and hopefully a few of the emotional ones as well.

From the box of bullets Lolo found the name of the guns they had been using. With Nyomi's phone he googled them hoping he could learn how to use them adequately. What he learned was music to his ears. The guns were easy to use. All he had to do was point and shoot. That is exactly what he told Nyomi. He only checked in case the first time they used them was a fluke or something.

Lolo had paused at the door before opening it. He really was reluctant to go, but he had to look out for them and listen to logic. They were two kids with two guns and two big bricks of dope. It would not have been smart to run around the city with all of that on them, nor would it have been smart to leave it behind unattended in the room. It still took Nyomi ten more minutes to convince him to leave. After all she was starving.

When he made it to the entrance of the motel, he saw the O.G. smoker from last night leaning up against a car reading the newspaper. The car was a Buick LeSabre that looked like it had seen better days. As long as it ran and wasn't stolen it would do.

"Excuse me, O.G.?" Lolo said as he approached him.

"What's good, lil Homie?" The old man responded, without taking his eyes off the paper.

"Is this your car?"

"What's it to you?" Again, he still didn't look up. "Well, if it is yours, and not stolen, I was wondering if you were trying to make a few bucks." This got the old man's attention.

He looked over at Lolo and sized him up. He put the paper down from his face.

"Look, youngsta. I don't have no time for games or no patience for bullshit. Are you serious or fucking with me?" The look on his face said he desperately needed Lolo to be serious.

"If you're up to it, I have a few errands to run. If you assist me with that, I'll give you $100 when we're done." Again the O.G. sized him up.

He thought it over for a second then said." If you put a little gas in it first, you got yourself a deal."

"I got you, O.G." They jumped into the car and drove to the nearest Chevron.

First, they swung by the IHOP on Veterans where Lolo bought some food for all of them. O.G.'s name was Chill Will. Him and Lolo ate as they drove back to the Capri and dropped Nyomi's food off to her.

Next, they hit up Tanforan Mall where Lolo dropped almost $2,000 on clothes and other accessories that they would need. He even got Chill Will a True Religion jean outfit, all black with the black and red Jordan Retros.

O.G. Chill Will was really feeling the youngsta's style.

"So, what's the deal, young playa? You and yo lil tender don't look old enough to be out here hustling, although I know how cruel the world can be. So, I know it's possible." He cut his eyes over at Lolo to get a feel off his vibe.

"Now the O.G. not trying to be all up in yo mix on no disrespectful shit, young Playa. I'm just trying to get in where I fit in."

Lolo sat quietly for a minute, digesting what the O.G. just said. All types of warning signs were going off inside of his head. Jennifer's words came back to him about the evil people in the street and how they manipulated and corrupted a person's mind.

He wasn't feeling negative vibes from Chill Will though. Everything about the O.G. seemed genuine. Lolo figured he'd test the waters a little.

"Nyomi is my world, O.G. She's all I got, and I'll put it all on the line for her. I can't say we're into anything too heavy. Life done hit us with a few blows and we're just trying not to get knocked down."

"I can dig that. Shit, I know about the blows that life can throw at you." Chill nodded his head giving confirmation to himself.

"Say O.G. can I ask you something that ain't none of my business?" Lolo asked as they pulled up to the Metro store.

"Shit, lil Homie, Chilly Willy ain't got nothing to hide cause ain't no shame in my game." Chill told him.

Neither of them made a move to get out the car yet.

102

"Okay. Do you get high O.G.?" Lolo made sure his tone was inquisitive instead of accusing.

"Hell yeah, I get high, lil Homie!" Chill smacked his left knee then let out a chuckle. "I thought you was gone ask a muthafucka something up close and personal. Anybody that knows the business can tell that Chilly Willy loves him some white bitch! Why, what's up?" This time he turned his head all the way so he could see what hype the lil Homie was on.

"You don't seem to have no job, so how you pay for it?" Lolo thought the question was innocent enough.

"Well shit, lil Homie, now you're getting personal." Lolo became a little nervous thinking he'd offended Chill.

Just when he opened his mouth to apologize, Chill added, "But like I said, I got no secrets cause I's ain't ashamed of what I do. Now seeing as your young ass is a little too young to be the police. Plus, you done hooked the O.G. up with this new outfit. I feel it's only right if I shoot it how it is with you, because I think it's more to it than you are letting on. Lil Homie, when that monkey is on my back, I do whatever I got to do to get his ass off me without jeopardizing or breaking my morals."

Lolo didn't know what monkey he was talking about. Nor did he know what morals were, but he didn't want to seem too ignorant. Instead, he hit him with another angle.

"O.G, Chill. I need you to tell me everything you know about dope." That was a good angle to come from, he figured.

"What kind of dope are you talking about?" Again, Lolo didn't know what kind of dope they had but didn't want to admit it.

With a serious look on his face Lolo looked at O.G. Chill Will and told him. "Every kind, O.G. Chill. I need you to tell me about everything." Lolo figured he would know what kind of drug they had back in the room.

"Sheeeiit! Come on in here, let's get you yo phone and then we'll rap. Cause what you are asking is gonna take some time for me

103

to break it all down to you." Chill knew his assessment of there being more to the kid was right.

Lolo was satisfied with that answer and said so. The two of them spent twenty minutes getting a phone for Lolo.

On the ride back to the motel Chill told Lolo everything he knew about heroin, which was just about everything. When they pulled up to the motel, they sat in the car in front of Lolo's room, while Lolo listened to Chill tell him everything there was to know about cocaine and crack.

Lolo paid Chill his $100 and asked him if they could finish the lesson a little later. He needed to get inside with Nyomi, he didn't want her to start worrying. Chill was cool with that. He was about to spend his time getting as high as Cooter Brown.

He told Lolo that he'd be parked out front in the same spot in an hour.

After Lolo carried the last bag into the room O.G. Chill pulled off. Nyomi was impressed with the clothes that Lolo picked out.

While she was going through all the bags Lolo walked over to the nightstand where her phone was and picked it up.

After programming each other's phone numbers into both phones Lolo went to the bathroom to take a piss.

Nyomi was impressed with how he was taking charge. When he finished, he came out the bathroom washed his hands and joined Nyomi who was sitting on the bed.

"Looks like you took care of everything." She told him as he laid down beside her.

Lolo and Chill had even made time to stop by the Grocery Outlet and pick up some snacks. He rolled over and grabbed a pack of gummi worms from out of the bag.

"You remember that old dude that walked up to the car last night?" he asked her while sticking a worm into his mouth.

"Yeah, I remember. What about him?" she asked while opening a pack of Skittles.

"I gave him a hundred to drive me around so I could get us what we needed. Anyway, I spent some time picking his brain about drugs. I didn't wanna say nothing about what we have so I had him tell me everything he knew about drugs, period. I'm supposed to meet back up with him in a minute to keep discussing it. But I think the package we got is cocaine."

Nyomi started to say something but decided against it. She already knew that it was cocaine from dealing with Von. She could tell that Lolo was proud of the work he was doing. She wasn't about to rob him of it by telling him she already knew.

"Now that you mentioned it, Von had something that looked just like it and he called it coke. I don't know how I forgot that." She hoped her acting skills were good enough to be convincing.

"It might be. How much you think it is?" he asked her.

Nyomi replied truthfully, "I don't know. I hope it's a lot though. I don't wanna sell my body no more." A sad look came across her face only to be replaced by a look of fear.

Her mental and emotional scars from the rape were still fresh in her mind as were her physical ones. She lowered her head as the tears cascaded down her pretty little face. She was tormented by the images that kept playing in her head.

Lolo leaned over and took her into his arms. "Shh! Shh! It's gonna be okay. Sssh. Come on Ny, don't cry, Babe." He spoke softly into her ear doing his best to comfort her and reassure her that she would heal, and things would get better. Every time she cried his heart shattered into a million pieces.

"It's not going to be okay. I'm ugly nowww!" Nyomi cried loudly in his arms.

"Ny, you will always be beautiful. Look at me," Lolo put his hand under her chin and gently lifted her face so that she was looking at him.

Through tear-stained eyes she timidly looked at him.

"Ny listen to me, I never judged you for what you were doing because you did what you had to do to survive. I respect you for it."

"As for what happened yesterday, no one can blame you for what that perverted son of a bitch did to you. Not even you. It wasn't your fault. When I first saw you, you were beautiful to me. When we made love, you were beautiful to me. And you are beautiful to me now. I promise you as long as you want me, I'll always be here." Lolo's words came from his heart and touched her soul.

"You're just saying that." She'd had too many let downs in her life for her to be able to trust someone's words that easily.

"I'm saying it because I mean it. I know I'm young Ny, but I love you. I know it's love because the only other time I knew it, was with Mama Jennifer. I'll never turn my back on you! Never!" Because he was serious his voice elevated a little.

But goddamn it, he thought bitterly, why it was so hard for her to understand. They were in this together. He would never abandon her.

"Lolo, for real? That's the nicest thing anyone has ever told me." The tears that fell now were tears of joy.

He kissed her softly on her cheek. Then he kissed her tears away. She turned her body completely facing him and he gave her a soft kiss on her lips.

Nyomi allowed her racing emotions to feed the kiss that went from soft and tender to passionate and strong. Her little heart was filled with so many emotions and she put them all in the kiss. Lolo did the same. Their kiss was so pure that their

106

young souls embraced in the kiss. Nyomi exhaled her essence and Lolo inhaled it. When he exhaled Nyomi greedily inhaled his life force.

When he finally broke the kiss she whispered, "thank you," softly into his ear.

Lolo felt himself becoming aroused during the kiss which was why he broke it off. He could only imagine what she was going through he didn't want to make matters worse by making a move on her because of his newfound sexual appetite.

He looked over at the clock on the nightstand and noted that it was getting close to time for him to meet O.G. Chill.

"Do you need me to stay with you instead of meeting up with the O.G.?" he kissed her on her forehead.

"No, it's okay I'll be fine. Just promise me you'll be safe." She told him while looking longingly into his eyes.

"You never got to worry about me, I'm always on my safety and security." Mama Jennifer used to always quote that phrase. "Safety and Security," to him and its meaning and importance.

Lolo stood up. An idea came to mind. He walked over to where they had the two bundles stashed. Removing one of them, he then unwrapped it and broke a nice little chunk off of it.

It took a little doing, but he was finally able to break a chunk roughly the size of a hardball. He placed it in a sandwich bag, cleaned up his mess and put the rest of it back where he'd gotten it from.

Next, he changed into one of the outfits he'd gotten earlier that day. A pair of black Guess Jeans with a matching black, grey Guess button down. A pair of black and grey Jordan Retro's, and all black Guess hoodie completed the outfit.

Lolo put the chunk of coke inside of the pocket in front of the hoodie with the all-black .38. He checked himself over once in the mirror. He was satisfied with his new look. He paused and thought to himself for a minute, then reached inside one of the Footlocker bags and pulled out an all-black Raider Nation baseball cap. He put it on and pulled it down low over his eyes.

"Okay, okay, Gangsta, do that shit then." Nyomi called out with a grin once he had everything just right.

Lolo walked over and bent down to give her a kiss.

"Lock the door, Babe. Call me if you need me." He grabbed his phone off the charger and walked out feeling like a new person.

CHAPTER TWELVE

The night sky was pitch black with barely a sliver of the moon visible in the cloudless sky.

True to his word, the Buick was parked in the same exact spot. Seeing it walked towards it. It was too dark to be able to look inside of the windows.

Lolo lightly knocked on the passenger's window once he was next to it.

"Jump on in, lil Homie." He heard Chill Will call out from inside.

When Lolo opened the door a cloud of putrid, sweet smoke slapped him in the face. It was the same smell from when Nyomi had him smoke the medicine.

He climbed in and closed the door. The Stylistics were playing softly on the radio. Lolo noted that it was a lot warmer inside of the car then outside in the fresh air. The smell was a lot stronger as well. Chill was leaned back in the seat grooving with the oldies. Sweat ran down his face but he didn't seem to mind.

"What you got going on, lil Homie?" Chill's face was nice and shiny from the sweat.

Looking at him Lolo noticed that his eyes were bugged out of his head. When Lolo looked in Chill's hand his suspicions were right. Inside of his hand was an identical pipe to the one Nyomi had.

"I'm back for more schooling, O.G. I see you're taking your medicine, huh?" he was pointing at the pipe.

"Medicine?" Chill chuckled. "Well hell, I guess you can call it that."

"What do you call it?"

"Well, this muthafucka here got many names, Crack, Cream, Butta, A-1, Yola, Sizzle, and that's just naming a few. I prefer to call it that white bitch, cause this shit is Satan's Candy and them white bitches are the devil." When he finished talking Chill smacked his lips loud like his mouth was dry. Then he reached inside the cup holder and came up with a 16oz can of Watermelon 4 Loco's beer and took a long swig.

"Nyomi called it medicine." Chill looked at him oddly for a while before saying.

"Well, I guess if you got real pain, whether physical or emotional, this bitch could ease that pain but it's only temporary. It's only a cheap fix never a solution, lil Homie." Although he couldn't imagine the little cutie pie that he'd seen smoking; Chill had to admit he had seen far worse in his life.

"Earlier when you were telling me about cocaine you said there was a whole other side to it. What is that?"

Lolo figured time was of the essence, so he'd best continue his lesson.

"Shit, lil Homie, we're talking about it. A muthafucka can take cocaine and hit it with a little bit of baking soda and turn that shit into crack. The best, most addicting drug in the world. Abracadabra! Poof!" He opened his closed hand, palm up showing a crack rock.

"Is that crack? How much is it? Why is it so addicting?" The questions rambled off immediately.

"Whoa! Whoa! Hold up, lil Homie. You gonna fuck my high up with all them questions. Hold on a minute." Lolo watched Chill break a piece off the rock he had and put it in his pipe and lit it up.

He pulled long and slow. His eyes were transfixed like he was in deep concentration. After about ten seconds he stopped pulling and inhaled deeply. Chill closed his eyes and blew the smoke out. His entire facial expression changed. He had a weird, goofy look on his face.

"How much did the rock in yo hand cost?" Lolo interrupted Chill's moment of hypnotic bliss.

"Shit, that's a dub piece. A dub is $20."

If that was $20.00 then Lolo assumed what he had, had to at least be a few hundred. He asked himself was he sure he wanted to take the risk.

A car drove by calling for Chill's attention. It was then that Lolo made his decision. He reached inside the hoodie and grabbed the bundle.

When Chill saw Lolo lift his hand up his eyes got big. "So, tell me O.G. how much is this?"

Chill grabbed the package out of Lolo's hand. He held it up eye level and began examining it. He turned it around and around sniffed it then squeezed it again.

"Damn, that's a solid chunk." he said to himself out loud.

"Just eyeballing it, I'd saying this was about an ounce, maybe more. Now if you sold it as is, you could get bout $800 for it right now. But if you bust it down to grams, you'll get 28 grams at $50 a gram, you're looking at $1,200 to $1,400."

"Now this is where the shit gets real. If you were to cook this soft and make it hard. You talking bout adding another seven grams. Off a solid 35-gram piece you could easily cut $2,000 or better, wait a minute." He unwrapped it and licked it. "This here's some good shit. You should be able to put a bigger spin on it. Whoever you got this from had to have gotten it straight off a brick. That's why it's so hard."

"What's a brick?" Lolo asked thinking they were getting somewhere.

"Cocaine comes in bricks, birds or kilogram. It's all the same thing. It's about the size of an old King James Bible. A kilo (key) got 36 ounces. Depending on how pure it is, you can flip anywhere from 42 to 56 ounces off of a kilo. Wholesale right now a key will cost you twenty-five thousand. Cooking it up rock for rock you could make fifty to seventy thousand dollars. And that's at sixteen hundred an ounce."

Lolo didn't know what to say. If O.G. Chill knew what he was talking about then he and Nyomi were rich. He was assuming that the two packages that they had were two kilos of cocaine or two keys. They were rich.

Before he realized what he was doing Lolo picked up the can of 4 Locos and took a drink. Chill burst out laughing.

After taking a moment to compose himself Lolo asked Chill. "How do you know who to sell it to, or where?"

This time Chill didn't chuckle nor laugh. He didn't want to make the lil Homie feel too bad. Instead, he lifted his hand and pointed at the Capri motel.

"Shit, lil Homie, you already at the best spot in the world. That motel is where the County Jail sends the muthafuckas that ain't got anywhere else to go. But them same muthafuckas know how to hustle up enough money to keep themselves high, believe that! Shit, look at me." Like he was proving his point Chill put his pipe to his lips and took a pull.

Lolo sat there in the passenger seat thinking about everything Chill broke down to him. What he heard was music to his ears. The question he was asking himself is, was everything that Chill just hit him with real?

Or was it just some bullshit?

What he did know was if selling dope meant he could take care of Nyomi and himself, she wouldn't have to prostitute. He was willing to take the risk.

CHAPTER THIRTEEN

Dirt lay on the bed trying hard to pay attention to the episode of Power that he was watching. Unfortunately, there was no use. No matter what he did he could not block out the noise. It didn't help matters any that the TV's volume control was set so that it couldn't go past a certain level.

Lately, the two of them had been arguing more and more and the arguments were getting worse. Twice Dirt heard loud crashing sounds like someone was throwing things. He tried to imagine what was going on, but too many scenarios played through his mind. The one thing that he knew was guaranteed or for certain was the fact that the two of them hated each other. If he were lucky, they would do him a favor and hurt each other and get it over with.

This time, the noise was louder than normal and there was cursing. Dirt craned his head to the left trying to hear better. He strained harder. Yes, he was certain of it now, they were arguing in the kitchen. Dirt hurried to get to the stairs to see what was going on. Midway up the stairs, he could hear the distinctive sound of pots and pans crashing like they were being thrown.

Dirt hoped that just maybe they would overdo it and one would kill the other. Or better yet that they would kill each other, but that would be too much going right. Dirt knew it wasn't going to happen.

Slowly he crept up the last four steps. He was being cautious, even though they were yelling so loud there was no way they would've heard him if he ran up the steps.

"You retched, backstabbing heathen! How dare you stand there and fix your blasphemous mouth to say such vile and disgusting things to your poor mother?" Mama Terry sounded like she was angry, yet on the verge of tears all at the same time.

"Oh! Vile and disgusting, huh? Tell me, Mother if saying the pastor's cock is vile and disgusting, why did you constantly force me to put it in my mouth! Huh?"

Another pot crashed into a cabinet. "Why did you force me to suck the pastor's vile and disgusting cock?" Rage filled Terrence's voice.

"You don't dare question what the good Lord put in the reverend's heart to help cleanse you of your devilish filth." Any signs of sorrow were forgotten when she spat the harsh words.

"It wasn't God that put the filth into his perverted heart, you cunt bitch! It was his own distorted lustful tendencies!" Terrence bellowed out.

Dirt couldn't believe what the fuck he was seeing, it couldn't be possible.

Removing his eyes from the keyhole. He thought back over the past eight months. There was no light down in the basement, so, his sight was terrible.

He thought about the time Mama Terry first came down into the basement beating him for no reason. The blows felt like they would kill him. She was a stout woman.

How about the time he first looked through the peephole and witnessed the two of them arguing? Actually, Dirt saw Terrence arguing, but never saw Mama Terry. He couldn't see her because the wall was in the way, obscuring her from his vision. He could only hear Mama Terry's strident voice.

Suddenly he remembered the time he was allowed up top to eat dinner. When he walked to the bathroom and saw past the wall and there was a big floor length mirror. There wasn't any room for someone to be standing there arguing with Terrence.

It all began to make sense; Mama Terry only came around when Terrence was gone. Dirt remembered thinking that it was odd that they were both the same size.

Dirt put his face back to the door and his eye back on the keyhole. His mind was desperately trying to analyze all the data it had stored over these months.

One thing for sure, Dirt could not deny what he was actually witnessing. Though he heard Mama Terry arguing with Terrence, it was Terrence himself doing all the yelling. Terrence was the only person in the kitchen. Terrence was Mama Terry and Mama Terry was Terrence. The entire time it was one person doing all of this to Dirt Bag.

Dirt Bag remained there stuck, unable to move a muscle. This muthafucka Terrence was suffering from some severe mental illness. He was schizophrenic, psychotic, and surely he had multiple personality disorders. Dirt mumbled to himself in disbelief. "This muthafucka is really unstable."

Suddenly, Terrence spun around and made direct eye contact with Dirt.

"Oh shit!" Dirt said as he halfway fell, halfway ran back down the stairs.

The basement door came crashing open. The gigantic form of Terrence filled the doorway momentarily before he stormed down the steps after Dirt.

"Damn heathen, Dirt Bag! Playing peek-a-boo, eavesdropping on me, huh? I'll teach you, you little Dirt Bag!"

Dirt noticed the peculiar look in his eyes. It was a faraway, distant look!

It wasn't Terrence, it was Mama Terry!

He had to go for it. He couldn't keep sitting idly by waiting for this deranged muthafucka in front of him to actually hurt him.

Dirt raced to the far-left corner of the basement. Mama Terry followed closely behind him. His adrenaline had Dirt's heart pumping rapidly. Overpowering him was out of the question. Dirt knew there was no way in hell he could overpower this mental patient. He would have to outmaneuver him. It was the only option.

117

"So, you wanna play games with Mama, do you, devil?" Mama Terry /Terrence lunged forward.

Dirt feigned left. It worked, she/he lunged in that direction. Dirt cut back like an NFL running back. He made the move holding his mouth open and tongue out like Michael Jordan. The maneuver caused Mama Terry/Terrence to stumble. Dirt took the steps two at a time. He reached the top of the landing in no time. He wanted so badly to look behind him to see where his assailant was. There wasn't time.

He covered the distance from around the corner in the kitchen to the front door in less than five seconds.

Placing his hand on the knob Dirt prayed it would open. Yes! He twisted the handle and snatched the door open. What the Fuck!

Standing there with the door open Dirt was staring at another door. A solid steel door that had been welded shut.

He spun around quickly!

"BAM!" Everything went black!

CHAPTER FOURTEEN

Sometimes in life a man must make a pivotal decision. A decision that he knows will alter the course of his life. It's a roll of the dice. Lolo took the risk and rolled the dice on Chill. That night they sat parked inside the Buick. It turned out the old man not only knew what he was talking about, but so far, Chill was turning out to be a real O.G. and a man of his word.

Lolo told Chill that night they were in the car that he was going to take a chance and trust him. At first, he didn't understand when Chill told him trust was a two-way street until Chill explained.

That night Chill took Lolo into Miriam's room. She was an Egyptian woman that Chill had a "Friends with Benefits" relationship with. Her genes leaned more towards the African side of her heritage than it did the Arabian. Her body was a true testament to that. However, her honey olive skin showed her Arabic side.

Looking at Miriam someone would never guess she was a drug addict. Her beauty was utterly breath-taking. She carried herself with respect and dignity. Standing 5'6" and weighing 185 lbs. Miriam not only favored Kim Kardashian in looks, she also would give Kim a run for her money in the body department. Only Miriam's physique was all-natural.

She had a microwave oven inside of her room that Chill used to get his Chef-Boy-R-Dee on. He had explained to Lolo the importance of cooking more dope at once. You would get a better flip, which meant more profit. Needless to say, Lolo went back to his room and retrieved nearly half of the brick.

Legend has it that the best chef to ever come from out the Bay Area was The Boi. However, O.G. Chilly Willy never got that memo. In his mind, he was the best.

Miriam and Lolo watched Chill as he performed his magic. Teaching Lolo everything that he knew in the process.

When he was done whipping up the cake (cake is a kilo of coke) he turned 16 ½ ounces of soft or powder coke into 25 ounces of hard crack cocaine. As bad as he wanted to take that spaceship ride to outer space, he knew if he blasted off, everything he worked for thus far would be ruined.

Chill took pride in everything he did. After making sure everything was done correctly and the solid slab cooled, he cut off a nice size rock and called Miriam over to him. "Listen now woman, this is business, not pleasure, you got me?" She nodded her head enthusiastically like a small child wanting a treat.

"Good, now take this and tell me what it does." Chill handed her the rock then leaned back with his arms crossed over his chest and waited, Lolo's anticipation was through the roof. He didn't know what he was waiting on. Nevertheless, he waited patiently.

Miriam licked her luscious lips as she loaded the straight shooter (pipe). Once the bowl was packed, she sparked her lighter and melted the rock. Finally, she put the pipe to her lips and lit it. Even while smoking she still had an aura of elegance about herself.

Dirt was eager. Chill waited patiently with a smile on his face. Miriam removed the flame from the pipe, finished pulling on it, then inhaled. Five seconds later she tilted her head backwards.

What happened next was amazing.

She blew the smoke out and immediately smacked her lips and took a deep breath as if she'd just sucked on a very sour lemon and grabbed her breast like she was having pains.

"Mmmm!" She moaned long and loudly. Afterwards she repeated the sour lemon move. Her eyes were closed, and her head hung down towards her ample breast. Suddenly she began squirming around in her chair like she had an invisible, irresistible itch.

"Mmm gawd damn! Daddy, this shit is fire!" Any and all sophistication or elegance was gone now as she reached up and grabbed both of her breasts and continued squirming around. The sounds she was making sounded like she was having an orgasm.

121

"Shyyiit! You gawd damn right that shit's fire. That's because Chilly Willy made it do what it do!"

The smile on his face expressed how much pride Chill actually took in accomplishing what he said he could do.

That was two days ago. In that time, Chill and Lolo sold four and half ounces all dimes ($10 rocks). The word was out in Redwood City that Chill Will had hooked up with a youngsta and they had that fire.

Lolo also found out over the two days that Chill Will used to be a cold hustlah back in the day. All his knowledge came in handy. First off, the manager of the motel was given $500 to turn a blind eye.

Lolo also let Chill Will know about the .38 so he would know that they had security. And together they ran the motel room like a trap house. The hours were from six o'clock in the morning until eleven o'clock and from nine o'clock until three in the morning.

Nyomi was so proud of Lolo, she was also happy that she didn't have to go out and work anymore. All she had to do was hold the ounces of crack that they weren't using.

Chill told Lolo with the stash being so close, they should never have more than an ounce with them in the room in case the police busted in, and they had to flush the dope. He also instructed Lolo to stash every $500.00 in the other room. Never have dope with a lot of money in the same place.

The only person besides them that knew the two rooms were adjoining was the manager. Normally, he reserved the room only for himself and he never rented the adjoining one.

Their set up was nice and it was lucrative. That first night Chill Will opted to take his payment in rocks. Miriam and he got high and did their thang. Last night however, Chill Will told Lolo that he wanted to sell his rocks once they closed-down shop.

The hustler was re-emerging in Chill Will, all it took was a taste of the hustle for him to get his mojo back. Lolo not only respected that, but he liked it as well. Not wanting Chill to burn himself out, Lolo told him instead of selling his rocks, the last half hour would be his time.

Lolo laid across the bed playing his Call of Duty video game on his phone. Nyomi was on her phone arguing with Von. Since he hadn't heard from her, Von decided to call and see what she was up to. After all, she still owed him his freebie and he was trying to collect.

The problem was Nyomi wasn't turning tricks anymore.

Von wasn't trying to hear any of that shit. He wasn't aware of the fact that she had been raped that night she called him for a ride. The sad thing was, even if he knew, Von would not have cared.

Nyomi had been pleading with him. Trying her hardest to get Von to understand. It wasn't working. Von was arguing with her instead of listening. The argument got to the point where he became irate and disrespectful.

Lolo tried to concentrate on his game to no avail. He was tired of having to listen to her beg and plead with the nigga. He could see that Von wasn't going to listen to reason, so Lolo didn't see any reason for her to continue explaining herself.

"Nyomi, that muthafucka not trying to hear shit you are saying. Hang up the phone." Nyomi looked over at Lolo.

She wanted to honor his request; she didn't want to defy or disobey him. Her level of respect for him grew because of the way he carried himself.

Her eyes pleaded with him to be understanding.

"Ny, come on Baby, hang up the phone. That nigga's not respecting you. Later, if he tries to listen to what you're telling him, maybe you'll get somewhere. As of right now, fuck what he is going through..." Lolo inherited the same no nonsense and zero tolerance to bullshit that his father T'Rida applied to his life.

123

Reluctantly, she listened to her man. Nyomi hung the phone up in Von's face while he was still ranting and raving.

Lolo saw the look of discomfort on his love's face. He asked her, why she was looking that way.

She said, "Von has a nasty temper, Daddy."

"Believe me, he'll get over it and any other problems his ass got." Lolo was sure of that.

Nyomi walked over to the bed and climbed in next to him and just like she knew he would do, Lolo put the phone down and pulled her into his arms. She loved laying in his arms, she always felt so secure.

Nyomi had been through so much shit in her young life. She often found herself thinking that God couldn't have given a damn about her, because if he did, he would've stepped in and intervened a long time ago.

"You wanna run and grab a bite to eat, Bae?" Lolo brought her out of her head with his question.

"Yeah, what are you in the mood for?" She honestly didn't want to leave out of his arms. But Nyomi did not care what they did, just as long as she was with him.

He gave her a kiss then stood up and told her, "I'll tell you what, let me take a quick shower and you decide while I'm in the shower."

"Okay, Bae."

Leaving her to her thoughts, he walked into the bathroom and hopped into the shower. His time sleeping on the streets wherever he could find a place to lay his head, taught Lolo how to appreciate the smaller things in life that most people took for granted every day.

There were times that he was forced to go months without bathing. Never had Lolo felt so miserable like he did during those times. As a result, sometimes he would shower three to four times a day if he had the chance.

Lost in his thoughts about Nyomi and what he wanted to do for her, Lolo did not hear the loud knocking on the door.

Nyomi was a special gift in his eyes, sent down from God as an answer to his prayers. She was his angel sent to comfort him and console him in his time of need and despair. He promised himself he would never forsake her or take her for granted. She may have been his angel, but he would make damn sure that he was the answer to her prayers.

Lolo could've sworn he heard yelling. He pulled the curtain back and stuck his head out of the water so he could hear better. This time he was sure Nyomi was arguing with someone. Lolo bounced out the shower. Wrapping a towel around his waist. He snatched the .38 off the back of the toilet where he had placed it. He snatched open the bathroom door and stepped out, pissed off!

"Bitch! Fuck, you mean I'm disrespecting your nigga? Fuck that little nigga and his feelings! Bitch, your ass owes me hoe, and I'm here to collect." Von was outside the doorway trying to force his way in while yelling at Nyomi, who was scared senseless, but refused to allow him inside the room without Lolo's permission.

"That's yo fucking problem right there. You got no respect, and you can't hear..." She was cut off in midsentence when she felt Lolo pull her backwards by her shoulder.

"What's up my Nigga? You got something you need to get off yo chest?" The door was blocking a portion of Lolo's body. Which meant Von was clueless to the .38 gripped tightly in his hand.

"Lil nigga, this don't got shit to do wit yo little ass! Gone and watch cartoons or something." The sight of Lolo standing in the doorway with a towel wrapped around his waist and dripping wet was comical to Von.

Lolo's bird-like chest rose up and down as he kept control of his breathing.

125

Von was a giant of a nigga, standing "6'2" and close to three hundred pounds. He was used to intimidating people and getting his way with his bullying tactics.

Lolo opened the door fully exposing himself, he was so focused on Von he didn't realize the towel had dropped. The chrome .38 gleamed in the sunlight drawing Von's attention.

"That's where you got me fucked up, my nigga. She is my business and anything that got to do with her is my business." Each time Lolo said, "my business", he used the .38 and pounded on Von's chest.

"Now you can get fucked up if you want to, and I can get all up in your shit. Or you can respect what she told you and keep it moving. I'll spell it out for you if you need me to. It's not that kind of party no more. Shit has changed, but you did do us a solid that day, so I don't have a problem papering you down for your time. But as far as she goes, that's not up for discussion anymore!" Lolo spoke with an aura of authority.

Nyomi stood there in silence with a smile on her face. Proud of her man as she listened to him handle the situation.

Von was in his 30's. He couldn't believe this little kid was getting at him on some gangsta shit like he was Wayne Perry, or some muthafuck'n body.

Von did not have to turn around to know that people were looking. He was used to it. He loved the attention usually. That's why he was loud and obnoxious. This time though, he was embarrassed, some little boy was pulling his hoe-card, and everybody was witnessing it.

He didn't have many options because the look in Lolo's eyes was a look Von knew well. It was a look that he didn't possess but had seen in the eyes of other people enough times to know what it was. It was the look of a killer. Von didn't know how it was possible, but the boy wasn't bluffing. He would use that pistol.

Just to save face, he talked shit as he nodded his head and walked backwards, but Von knew in his heart, he wasn't going to bust a grape in a food fight.

O.G. Chill, he watched the scene unfold. When Chill Will first heard the banging on the door, he thought it was the police. When he heard the arguing he was concerned for his lil Homie and stepped outside with his hand inside his jacket pocket, ready. Chill was gripping the handle of the all-black .38 that Lolo had left with him.

Once Von pulled off, Chill Will and Lolo made eye contact. A silent understanding was received.

Back inside the room, Nyomi ran and jumped into Lolo's arms as soon as he shut the door.

"I love you Daddy." she kept repeating over and over again as she kissed him all over his face.

Nyomi had never in her life had someone defend her or represent for her. Lolo put it down though to the fullest. In that moment, her love for him reached a level that would neva die.

After relishing the affection, she was giving him Lolo released her. "Let me throw some clothes on and we can get up out of here and get you something to eat." He playfully smacked her on her ass before walking towards his clothes.

Once he was dressed Lolo checked in on Chill Will to see how things were looking.

"Sheeiit. lil Homie, I'm down to under our last quarter on this ounce. You might wanna toss me another one before you two get out of here," Chill Will informed his young boss with pride.

"Gawd damn Chill, let me find out you over here doing magic tricks with the work and shit." Lolo joked.

"You ain't said nothing but a word, lil Homie. Abracadabra! Bitch be gone!" Chill Will moved his arms around mimicking a magician.

127

"Okay. Look, check it out. Whatever's left why don't you keep it for yourself. I'mma grab this shit for you to whip up. Might as well get ahead of the game Chill-Boy-R-Dee, before the rush kick up."

"Now that's thinking like a hustlah! I like that." Chill Will could tell his young protégé was gone take the Bay by storm. He could see the signs that Lolo was on his way to being a major player in the streets.

"Oh yeah! Here." He dug into his pocket. "I didn't want to disturb you since you was with the Queen. That's $2,700. That came within the last hour you were tied up." he said handing the cash over.

"Alright, bet! Give me one second." Lolo dipped back into the other room.

He went to the spot that he had the rest of the dope stashed. There was still the whole bird along with the rest of the other half. Lolo paused momentarily making up his mind. He snatched it all up. Lolo left about four ounces of the half brick in the room just in case.

"Like you said, big Homie. Respect is a two-way street that leads to trust. This here is about one and a quarter bird. We only got bout four onions left. All that I have materialistically in this world is in your hands, big Homie. Let's get it!" It did not go over Chill Will's head that Lolo called him big Homie instead of O.G. Although both were terms of endearment, being called big Homie meant that Lolo now looked up to Chill Will and held him in higher respect.

The hustle that was reborn in Chill Will wanted to ask Lolo why he was leaving out the last four pack. But the "G" in him told him not to push it.

"You want anything to eat, big Homie?"

"Where y'all headed?" Chill Will really was not tripping off of food. Hustling was his new high and that's all he cared about, but he had to think of Miriam.

128

"Shit, big Homie... I'mma let the Queen decide."

"Well shit, just bring something back for Miriam. You know the O.G., I'm good." Chill Will was in his groove and nothing was going to fuck that up.

He reached in his pocket to give Lolo the money for the food. Feeling good that once again he was able to reach into his pocket and pull out a nice size meat loaf. Damn, meeting a 10-year-old boy was the most profound thing to ever happen in his life.

"Come on, big Homie don't do me like that. You know I got you." One thing Lolo respected about Chill Will, he never took things for granted and he never tried to get over on him. Lolo tested him on a few occasions but the O.G. was solid.

Lolo dapped up his new, big Homie and locked the connecting door back. Nyomi sat patiently on the bed while her man took care of his business.

"Let's go, Mama." Lolo didn't know it, but he'd locked her down. He had a "Ridah" for life.

Outside they hopped into Chill's Buick. Chill Will had been letting them use the car because Nyomi looked old enough to be driving. As they were pulling off Lolo instructed her to pull up by Miriam, whose job was to post up and direct traffic.

"Shop closed, Miriam. We're about to grab something to eat and the big Homie bout to bake a cake." Lolo told her when she walked up to the car.

"Okay, honey. You two be safe out there." Miriam was glad to be able to take a break. Chill Will wouldn't allow her to fuck around while they were hustling. She needed a hit bad!

Nyomi pulled off into the night headed for her new favorite restaurant, The Cheesecake Factory was calling her name.

CHAPTER FIFTEEN

Dirt was waking up. He had a headache that was out of this world. At first, he didn't know what had happened to him. The more he awakened the more his memory started coming back. Slowly but surely.

He thought he'd finally gotten his chance at escaping, but in the end, he was a fool. When he spun around from the steel door Mama Terry cold cocked him in the jaw, knocking him out.

Unbeknownst to Dirt, he had one hell of a concussion from the blow. Slowly he began opening his eyes. He sensed a presence in the room.

"Who's there?" Dirt called out.

"Now look at what you've gone and did Dirt. I trusted you and Mama told me that you tried to get away." Terrence slowly came into view from the right side holding something in his hands.

Dirt tried to get a better look, but he couldn't move. For the first time he realized that he was strapped down to the bed. He tried desperately to shake the straps loose, but it was useless. He was strapped down good and tight.

"You know when I was a kid there was this movie out named Misery. It was my favorite movie." Dirt wasn't trying to hear any of that bullshit. He was wiggling his hardest, trying to get free.

"It was a movie about a psycho that rescued her favorite author from a crash only to keep him captive and strapped to a bed..." Lolo knew the movie well. Mama Jennifer used to watch it all the time.

"When the author, James Caan played, tried to get away, she was forced to break his ankles in order to teach him a lesson..." Holy Shit! Dirt remembered that scene very well. She fucked dude's feet up with the sledgehammer.

"W-w-what. W-w-wait! Wait! Terrence, she's lying. That cunt bitch is lying. I never tried to escape!" Dirt was beyond desperate.

If he allowed Terrence to break his ankles there was no telling how long, he would be trapped in that fucking basement.

"Now why would she go and do that for?" The sledgehammer was resting against his left shoulder.

"I heard the two of you up there fighting. She was throwing pots and pans at you. When I came up there to help you, she knocked me out because I took your side. That cunt bitch is lying." Dirt hoped somehow that by calling her the name Terrence used when he was mad at her, it would get his attention.

It looked like it was working for a while because Terrence was blinking his eyes like something was bothering them.

Dirt did not know if it was actually working but he didn't have shit to lose, so he kept it up.

"Terrence, she saw us getting close and becoming friends. So, she's trying to come between us. Don't let that cunt bitch win, big Homie! Terrence, we all we got." Terrence was shaking his head trying to clear his thoughts.

"And I shall smite out every living male of their bloodline down to the last one in order to show that I am the Lord thy God. The God of Israel!" It wasn't Terrence anymore.

Right before Dirt's eyes Terrence became Mama Terry.

"You foul, retched, Dirt Bag! How dare you blaspheme me with your sewer tongue?" She raised the sledgehammer high above her head, getting ready to crash Dirt's feet that were separated by a 2x4 piece of wood like in the movie.

Dirt's heart raced 200 miles per hour out of pure fear! He didn't know what to do.

Dirt closed his eyes so he wouldn't have to witness the mutilation.

"Terrence, I-l-love you brotha! Please don't do it bro, I love you!" He didn't know what else to do, or to say. He opened one of his eyes just barely to see if what he said was working.

Mama Terry swung the sledgehammer down in an arch! Just before the sledgehammer connected with Dirt's foot, Terrence appeared.

The blow never came. Dirt was scared at first for fear that she was taunting him. Waiting to strike when he opened his eyes.

"Dirt, you really mean that? Am I your big Homie, Dirt? Do you love me?" Dirt may have doubted God at some points in his young life while going through all the things he'd been through. But right then he knew that God answered prayers. This was a fucking miracle!

Hands down!

"Big Homie, it's you! Yeah, I love you man! I wouldn't play bout that shit. I would die about this shit!" Dirt was so happy to still be in one complete piece, a single tear rolled down his cheek.

Terrence saw the tear and mistakenly took it as a sign of sincerity. He tossed the sledgehammer across the room, and then began untying Dirt's restraints.

When he finally got the last strap free, Dirt jumped up and hugged Terrence. He was genuinely grateful that the sick, demented, fuck. Hadn't crushed his feet with the sledgehammer.

"It's okay, lil Homie. I won't let that cunt bitch harm you ever again." Terrence sounded like a mentally challenged adult with the mind of a child.

"Thank you, big Homie." Dirt was beginning to feel weird being all hugged up with this muthafucka. But he would play the fuck out of an Oscar winning performance if that's what the fuck it took.

"We gotta be careful, lil Homie. She's going to be mad that I untied you. So, we gotta watch her cause she's going to be up to something." Terrence paused like he had forgotten something.

Dirt just watched him, hoping Mama Terry wasn't trying to come back.

"I gotta make dinner, lil Homie, I gotta make dinner." He was acting weird.

"Big Homie, can we eat dinner together tonight? Maybe if we're together she won't mess with us." Dirt was beyond desperate. Shit… something had to give.

"Yeah, that sounds good, lil Homie. I'll come back for you once it's done." Terrence turned around and left out of the basement.

Dirt collapsed on the bed, exhausted. Between his fear and anxiety, all his energy was gone. He knew this shit was destroying him little by little. No matter what the outcome Dirt had to try to get out of here tonight.

From all of what Mama Jennifer told him about his father and real mother, neither one of them were quitters. They both died fighting to the death. And so would he!

Dirt stood up to check and see if his screwdriver was still under the mattress. It was. He grabbed the screwdriver and tucked it inside of his pants. Terrence had bought a few outfits for him from the Salvation Army a couple of months back. Dirt didn't care too much about it back then, but right now he was thankful for it. There was not really much more he could do but wait. He knew that anxiety would only make time go by slower than normal.

With that in mind he turned the TV on and searched On-Demand for another episode of Power. Ghost' son had been hanging around Kanan not knowing that he was the enemy. Terrence came back down to get Dirt, right around the time Ghost' son passed out on the couch from drinking too much syrup.

"Dinner's ready, lil Homie." Terrence called from the bottom step.

"Hey, big Homie. You think we could eat down here and finish watching Power?" Dirt was hoping that kissing a little ass would go a long way.

"Why not? I love Power. Let me go get the plates." Terrence's answer actually shocked Dirt. He'd wanted that answer but wasn't expecting it. If Dirt could get Terrence distracted by the show, then just maybe he could get close enough to stab him in the neck with the screwdriver.

Terrence came back with the food. Two identical plates with heaping mounds of food on them. He handed Dirt his plate then sat down on the right side of Dirt.

"Did you restart it?" he asked Dirt. "You know I did, big Homie."

They say this is a big rich town / I just happen to come up hard / bright lights big city I gotta make it.

The theme music from Power began playing on the TV.

"Big Homie, you forgot the drinks. You want me to run and grab them?" Dirt's little mental wheels were at work spinning inside of his head.

"Shit!" Terrence sat his plate on the TV stand. "Okay, pause it before it starts, I'll be right back."

Terrence shot up the stairs like lightning. Looking at Terrence's plate Dirt told himself it was now or never! He had actually caught the muthafucka off guard. He was still deciding what to do next when he heard Terrence coming down the staircase. Terrence handed Dirt a cup and sat down and picked his plate back up. He cut a chunk of the meat log with his fork and brought it to his lips. With his mouth wide open he paused and raised one eyebrow like the wrestler The Rock. He looked over at Dirt who was chomping down on his food like a runaway slave at a banquet. Terrence shrugged his shoulders and shoved the forkful into his mouth.

Neither one of them were paying any attention to Tasha on the screen as she yelled at Ghost. They were too busy fucking their plates

135

up. It almost seemed like they were competing with each other to see who would finish first. Of course, that was a competition that Dirt didn't stand a chance at winning. After all Terrence was a grizzly bear.

"You want some seconds, lil Homie?" It had been many years since the last time that Terrence was this happy.

People often misunderstood him. All he ever wanted was a friend to play with. Not how his mother and the pastor played with him. That was evil. He just wanted to be a normal boy and do the things normal boys did.

"Hell yeah, big Homie! Thanks." Dirt wondered if he did so tonight. Judging from the way he looked at Dirt when he put the fork in his mouth, Dirt was guessing he did. Terrence grabbed the plate that Dirt handed him. He licked his lips and blinked his eyes. After that he stood up to go to the kitchen.

And then......

CHAPTER SIXTEEN

It began raining just over twenty-minutes ago. The night darkness plus the torrential downpour lessened his visibility a great deal. The Watcher has been sitting in the same spot for hours now. Watching and observing. Trying to make sense out of all that he was seeing.

When the two of them first began to drive off, he watched as the car stopped to talk to the foreign chick. Once they pulled off, he pulled up hoping to solicit some information from her.

Up close he was able to see the tell-tale sign of a junkie in need of a fix. So, he just knew he would get his answers. Unfortunately for him, she had stitch lips. Upset, he drove off faking like he was leaving. Once he'd came back around however the foreigner had disappeared.

She popped back up a little while later. Perched on her spot like an owl observing the forest floor. Only to constantly watch his car. When she pulled out her cell phone and made a call, he got nervous. When he spotted the man whom she had to have called come out and she pointed at his car, he got out right scared and pulled off.

An hour later he pulled back up making sure to park out of her sightline. The problem with that, however, was his view of the inside of the motel was obscured. However, he sat patiently and waited. This was by far not his first time being on some sneaky shit. Sure, enough his patience paid off a little while later. They pulled back into the motel about thirty minutes ago, just before the storm came.

His original idea was to do some female shit and damage the car. That was until he learned what he had learned.

The motel was a gold mine and the Watcher knew it..
He saw dope fiend after dope fiend come walking hungrily up

to the motel. Finally, he stopped one of the dope fiends, a fat white woman with acne and scars all over her neck and face.

"Hey, lil mama. I got $50 for you if you can tell me what's popping." he told her.

Her greed compelled her to get the money. The ugly scowl that was just on her face moments ago was replaced with a warm toothless smile.

"What chou trying to find out sugar?" Her breath smelled like shit and wet mold.

The Watcher almost threw up his lunch the moment the God-awful smell seeped from her mouth.

"I'm seeing addict after addict hit that motel up. A couple of the same ones done came by three or four times. Who got it popping up in there?" The way he worded the question the Watcher sounded like the police.

The dope fiend secretly tucked the rocks she had bought into her pocket out of sight.

"That's easy honey. Chill Will and that little boy he got with him got that fire." She bragged like she was the one who had it.

"The lil boy?" he mumbled to himself. "What lil boy you talking about?" he asked her.

"Sugar, there's only one lil boy round here's and that's the little cutie that's shacked up with that other girl."

When she said this the Watcher couldn't believe his ears.

"You talking bout the two I seen earlier driving in that Buick?" he questioned.

"That's them honey. They got some shit up in there that taste like the shit from back in the 80's." Remembering the dope that she had in her pocket. The dope fiend stuck out her dirty hand.

"Now if that's it Sugar, I'll take my money and leave.

Unless it's something else you need." When she said this. She had the nerve to lean over so that her musty tit was in his face and licked her crusty lips.

He never had the intentions on paying her to begin with. But now the bitch was just being disrespectful.

He lifted his shirt revealing the big ass .45 automatic that was sitting on his lap.

"Bitch, you betta get cho stank ass outta my face. Bitch, don't nobody want no diseased-ass pussy." With a mug on her face the dope fiend scurried away and quickly blended into the night.

Yeah, the Watcher knew exactly what the fuck he was going to do. He's been doing it ever since that time he'd gotten into that trouble at the Good Guys Store he used to work for.

Punching in the numbers he put the phone to his ear and listening to it ring.

"911 emergency." The dispatch operator came over the line. "What's your emergency?"

"Uh yeah I'm at the Capri Motel on El Camino. I just witnessed a guy fondling a little boy inside one of the motel rooms."

"Sir did you happen to see which room he took the boy into?" The female dispatcher asked.

"Yes, I did." He gave the dispatcher the room number that Lolo and Nyomi was staying in.

"Attention all units, this is dispatch. We have an active...."

Once he heard the call go out over the radio, the Watcher, Von Jack, knew his work was done. Smiling like the bitch nigga he was, he pressed end on his cell phone and dropped it into his passenger seat.

That would teach muthafuckas to disrespect him. He wished he could see the look on the little muthafuckas face when the police raided the room and took them all to jail.

Hopefully, they wouldn't take Nyomi because he had something in store for that little bitch! How dare she talk to him like he was some simp-ass nigga?

Von would teach that little bitch a lesson. By the time he was done with her, the little bitch would've wished she had given it to him freely.

**** N. D. ****

Lolo and Nyomi were laid across the bed. He was on his back, and she had her head resting on his little chest. He was gently stroking his hand through her long silky hair. If this moment was all that life had to offer, Lolo was cool with that. His bae was in his arms resting after returning from the Cheesecake Factory. Where they got their eat on uninterrupted.

Even though Chill Will said he didn't want anything Lolo made sure that they brought back two plates of that bomb ass food. After he dropped the food off, he stopped in the office to take care of the manager. Then he retired to the room with his lady. The two of them have been laid up the way they were now ever since.

"Thomas, I Love you Bae." Nyomi spoke into his chest.

Before Lolo got a chance to respond, there was loud banging on the door. The first thing Lolo did was snatch up the .38 from off the night- stand. He didn't know who it was, but he was ready to protect what was his.

What he wasn't ready for was… "San Mateo, Sheriff's Department! Open the door before we break it down!"

This caused Lolo to jump into action. He bolted up from the bed and made sure the connecting door was locked. Next, he tucked his .38 inside of his waistband.

141

"Come on Ny." She was right behind him. Her heartbeat thrumming to the same cadence as his.

She didn't know what he had planned but she believed in him. As she got off the bed, Lolo grabbed the four ounces from the tuck spot and put them in his drawers.

The only thing that was on Lolo's mind was the nigga they killed in the abandoned house. His mind never once went to the little operation they had going on or anything else.

The loud banging came again as Lolo entered the bathroom. There was a window in the wall above the bathtub. He'd already had this planned. It was because of his plan that the window remained open. More pounding came from the front. Lolo climbed out the window. Once he climbed through, he would help Nyomi climb down.

"Okay." she told him after he explained it to her.

When he swung his second leg through the window, the plastic bag with the four ounces in it dropped out of his underwear and in the bathtub.

"I got it!" Nyomi told him.

"Fuck it Ny! Let's go." Lolo had already dropped down from the window. He couldn't see Nyomi, and this scared him.

When Nyomi bent down to retrieve the bag. The front door came crashing in. Sheriff's deputies stormed the small room.

Nyomi stood up with the bag in her hand. She looked out of the window with a sad look on her face. "I love you Lolo!" A tear slowly rolled down her cheek. "Ny, no! Ny!" But it was too late.

Nyomi reached up and slammed the window down, closing it shut.

Right then the bathroom door came crashing in. "Freeze! Don't move!"

"Hands above your head! Let me see your hands!" The deputies were yelling so many different commands all at once that she didn't know what to do.

"Ny!" Lolo shouted again.

"Fuck!" he shouted, why did she do that... he needed to know.

He chastised himself for going through the window first, but he had to. He told himself what if they would've ran into a problem? He would've had to deal with it.

But why in the fuck would she just do that? It was fucking with his head. He knew he had to take off, but he couldn't take his eyes off the window. His mind was telling him that Ny would need him. If they both were captured, he wouldn't be able to do shit to help her out. Reluctantly Lolo took his eyes off the window and sprinted down the dark wet alley. He ran in the direction of the front of the motel.

Once Lolo got to the front, he saw that the entire front of the motel was blocked off. He desperately wanted to see Nyomi, to make sure she was okay. He stood just off to the front mouth of the alley, getting soaked by the rain.

"Go check around the back. The caller said something about a little boy." A deputy called out to another.

Lolo didn't wait. He climbed the fence and went in the direction of the shadows. Blending in with the night he watched the Sherriff's deputies do their thang, while the rain came down and did its thang.

Lolo figured he'd wait until they left and hook up with Chill Will. He really didn't have any other option because since Chill Will left them with the keys to the Buick. Lolo stashed all of their money inside of the speaker box that was in the trunk.

Everything that he had to his name literally was with Chill Will. All Lolo could do is hope that his big Homie wouldn't cross game and fuck him over. It was a big gamble young Lolo took

143

entrusting the O.G. But things were going so fast and everything was looking so good, Lolo followed his instincts about Chill Will.

Deputies were swarming all around searching the area. Some had walked literally five feet in front of Lolo. If they would've shined their light in his direction, they would've seen him.

"Stay there, Hoffman. Sarge says someone reported seeing somebody climb out of the back window and take off down the alley. There's a possibility that the perp may still be in the vicinity. The Sergeant says he wants you to call in the K-9 units." Lolo couldn't see the Deputy who was calling out the directive.

"Alright 10-4. Dispatch this is…" Lolo was able to see the Deputy who received the directive though. Deputy Hoffman was directly in front of Lolo standing on the opposite side of the fence while she radioed the order in.

Lolo couldn't fucking believe it. The saying was "When it rains it pours." Well hell, it was surely coming down on him both metaphorically and literally.

There was nothing he could do but get the fuck out of the area before they found him. With the weight of the world on his shoulders he hunched his shoulders and disappeared into the stormy night.

CHAPTER SEVENTEEN

Dirt held his breath. He did not want to get his hopes up only to be let down. He damn sure didn't want to jump the gun.

He watched Terrence blink his eyes in confusion. Watched as he swayed left then right. And then it happened. Terrence fell face down on the concrete floor with a mighty crash!

Immediately Dirt got the fuck off his ass and jumped into action. When he jumped up, he bumped into the TV stand sending it crashing to the floor as well.

He didn't give a fuck!

He ran to the shackle that was lying in a pile on the floor. His heartbeat racing a million miles a minute. He even broke out into a nice nervous sweat. Wasting no time, he managed to get the shackle around one of Terrence meaty ankles.

After locking the shackle in place, he frantically began rummaging through Terrence's pockets looking for the key. The entire time he searched, unaware that he was holding his breath.

It took all the strength that Dirt could muster up to be able to roll Terrence's massive body over. When he finally got that done. Dirt found the shackle key inside of Terrence's front right pocket. Once he retrieved the key and took a couple of steps backwards Dirt was able to take two massive much needed deep breaths.

Finally, the nightmare was over! At least for him it was.

Feeling his confidence, in his now pretty big chest. Dirt cocked his left leg back for an NFL like field goal kick and kicked the fuck out of Terrence's jaw. Had he not been knocked out already, the kick would have surely knocked him out.

Pulling the screwdriver out of his waistband Dirt shot up the basement stairs. Holding the screwdriver, the same way Michael Myers held his knife Dirt was prepared to bring the hounds of hell to this bitch.

After clearing the first floor which only consisted of the kitchen, dining area, bathroom, and living room, Dirt more cautiously made his way to the second landing.

Once he reached the top of the landing, he'd already determined he would die before he allowed himself to mess this chance up and be recaptured. All sorts of thoughts swam through his mind.

If he was thinking he would've grabbed one of the big ass butcher or carving knives from out of the kitchen. But Dirt wasn't thinking, he was operating on pure instincts fueled by adrenaline.

The first door he came to was on his left. Twisting the handle as slowly as possible as not to make any noise Dirt opened the door. The room was empty. Upon his first inspection he saw two flat screens mounted on the ceiling above the bed. One of ones hanging over the bed was actually on. Now was not the time, however, to find out what it was showing.

The door opposite that room and a little farther down the hall was next. Holding his breath, Dirt opened that door in the same manner as he did the first. That room was empty as well. However, something was on the bed.

Something inside of him screamed for him to investigate. Yet, making sure no one else was in the house was Dirt's first priority. The next door was on the same side of the hallway as the one he just left out of.

He opened the door and stepped inside ready for whatever he may find. This room was empty as well, just like the last room. But he noticed there was something on the bed. The odor in the room was similar to a New York City abandoned subway station.

TV's were mounted in this room in the same exact manner as the first room. Dirt made his way inside the room. Right off, he could tell that it was a female's room. From the bedding and the pink sheer cover that was on top of the main dresser.

Stepping forward he thought surely his eyes had to be playing tricks on him. For on the bed laid an old, decayed skeleton. He assumed it was a woman because the bones were inside of a dress. One of them old dresses that the elder church moms wear on Sunday morning.

In the center of the dress where the chest should've been, was a huge iron spike standing straight up. Dirt could only imagine that when she was stabbed with the huge spike it was done with so much force that it went clearly through her, the mattress, and the box spring. The thick layer of dust on the spike told Dirt that it must've been there for some years. He figured it must have been Mama Terry's bones in the bed.

Looking around his attention was on the few pictures placed on one of the nightstands. They were of an older woman perhaps in her late forties or early fifties.

In one of the pictures, she was standing next to a pastor, who had one of his arms draped around her shoulder? Both she and the pastor were smiling widely. There was no warmth or love in either of their expressions. No welcoming sense of care. Instead, they appeared eerie and sadistic. Just looking at the picture gave Dirt the creeps.

He made his way out of the room and backtracked into the other room. Walking up to the bed it was identical to the room with the female skeleton. This skeleton however was wearing a pair of slacks, so he figured it was a man. Upon further inspection he noticed there was a clergy collar up at the head of the skeleton.

Dirt wasn't sure who the pastor was. His only guess was it had to be the pastor that used to molest Terrence in the picture with the woman. The woman had to be none other than Mama Terry he figured.

His assumptions also told him that more than likely it was Terrence who killed both of them by driving the massive six- foot iron spikes straight through their hearts.

Back inside Mama Terry's room, curiosity had gotten the better of Dirt, so he pressed power on one of the remote controls.

149

The TV came to life and the scene was of the pastor in the pictures with a little boy who could not have been any older than Dirt himself. Dirt could tell the little boy was terrified from the tears that he cried and the way he kept trembling. While the sick pastor forcibly instructed him to perform all sorts of God-awful sexual acts on him. The sight made Dirt sick to his stomach.

Dirt heard a woman's high-pitched voice reprimanding the little boy she referred to as "Dirt Bag" or "Terminator", any time he didn't immediately do what the sadistic pastor instructed him to do.

Dirt couldn't take much more of watching the grotesque shit on the screen. He flicked it off and hit power on another remote. The TV lit up and the scene was the same as the first only it was with the little boy and Mama Terry. She forced him to perform oral sex on her while someone outside of the view spanked the little boy on his buttocks with a long paddle.

The two TV's above the bed on the ceiling were both live images of the basement. He left out of Mama Terry's room and went into the very first room he came upon. In there he turned on all four TV's, one was a regular TV and it was tuned into CNN News. The second was the same video of the pastor and the little boy. The third TV was a live feed of outside the house in the front yard. It had a perfect clear view of the gate to enter the property. Just like with Mama Terry's the last screen was a live feed of the basement.

On his way out of the room Dirt found a ring of keys on the dresser along with his black snub-nosed .38 special. Terrence took it off him the night that he knocked Dirt out on the side of the house. Dirt picked both up off the dresser. The .38 went inside of his waistband while the keys went inside of his front pocket before he made his way back down to the kitchen.

The refrigerator was fully stocked. The problem was Dirt didn't know how to cook too many things. He pulled all the works out of the fridge to make cold cuts. He just loved cold cut sandwiches.

Before starting his sandwiches, he got a pot out and began boiling water. It took Dirt a good ten minutes to make three turkey sandwiches with lettuce, tomato, cheese, pickles, mustard, and mayonnaise. Inside of the fridge on the bottom shelf was a twelve-pack of Sunkist Sodas, Dirt grabbed two.

Thirty minutes later he was good and full. For some reason he thought of the big mirror in the front and went and stood in front of it. The months of doing pushups and all the good food that Terrence was feeding him had added fifty plus pounds onto his skinny frame. Taking his shirt off and flexing. He looked nothing like the kid who was starving in the dumpster eating whatever he could.

Instead, he was seeing a miniature body sculpting, dark eyes, vengeance seeking Dirt. The dark mystery that his eyes took on told a tale of heartache and pain that the average twenty-four-year-old had never endured.

Hearing a hissing sound drew his attention back to the kitchen. Walking in that direction, Dirt had forgotten all about his boiling water. Water that was boiling over and running down to the electric elements on the stove causing it to his and quickly evaporate.

This time it was Dirt who had the sadistic smile and the spark of mischief in his eyes. He turned the burner off, grabbed the pot and then descended the stairs to the basement.

"Oh, When the Saints go marching in, oh when the Saints go marching in…Oh Lord I want to be in that number…. oh, when the Saints go marching in." he sang the same exact church hymn that Mama Terry sang that first night.

Terrence was still laid in the exact same place that Dirt left him. He was going to love this shit. "Thank You Jesus!" Dirt shouted at the top of his lungs. "And the One who comes after me whose sandal strap I am unworthy to tie, He shall baptize you with the Holy

Spirit!" After he spoke the last word, he threw the pot of scalding hot water right onto Terrence!

"Lazarus awaken!" The sound that erupted out of Terrence's mouth was somewhere between a grizzly bear's mighty roar and wounded dog.

Dirt lit up with pure bliss. He smiled as he watched Terrence roll around on the ground in pain.

"How's it feel, Terminator?" he teased and tormented.

"D-D-Dirt I-I- th-thought we were f-friends?" Terrence sounded like a scared little schoolgirl.

"Friends? Naw, nigga I saw all the sick twisted perverted shit you were planning to do me!" Dirt shouted loudly, his voice echoing in the basement.

"N-Not me Dirt. It was them! That cunt-bitch and her pastor." Terrence was actually crying by now.

Blisters formed over his body in the places where the water scorched his skin.

"See, the fucked-up thing is I know what they did to you.

So, I know you're fucked up on many levels. My heart goes out to you my nigga, it does. That was some fucked up shit for real. But you see the problem is you took care of them. I see your handiwork upstairs."

"No matter how fucked up your head is. It was you my nigga, that did all that shit to me. You, my nigga… not them!"

Wham!

Without warming Dirt cracked Terrence across the head as hard as he could with the copper bottom pot.

Terrence fell over to his side more out of misery than out of pain.

"I'm sorry Dirt, I am. They did this to me. It was them." he cried balling himself up in a little ball.

"I know. I know, it was them but trust me this gonna be all me." Dirt turned around and walked out of the basement.

CHAPTER EIGHTEEN

Lolo was lost, tired, hungry, and paranoid. It had been three nights since Nyomi was locked up. That night he was so scared of the police getting him, that he just ran and ran and ran until he couldn't any longer.

By then he was lost and so paranoid that every set of headlights he thought was the police. That only made him run, jump, and hide wherever he could. The end result by the time the rain began letting up it was almost sunrise, and he was totally without a doubt lost. Lost without a clue as to what he was going to do.

His clothes were completely drenched from the downpour. Not only was he wet and cold but the clothes felt like they weighed just as much as cement blocks.

Finally, he saw an apartment complex that had carports. When he went over there thinking he was finally going to get out of the rain, it had motion lights. The damn things came on and wouldn't turn off. To make things even worse there was a barking ass dog nearby that just wouldn't shut the hell up.

Poor Lolo was scared beyond belief and barely holding it together, so he left. The next couple of days were just as messed up as that first night.

Lolo was on the verge of giving up. Just dropping down right there on the ground and giving up. To hell with the white girl with the funny walk and bad breath.

"What was her name?" he asked himself. "What was it? What was it?" He was trying hard to remember.

Bingo!

"Hey Misty! Hey Misty!" he shouted.

The white girl looked around trying to see who had called her.

Lolo ran as fast as he could in the soiled heavy clothes, across the street. He was oblivious to the many cars honking their horns at him. The scene he caused got her attention and she looked in his direction trying to concentrate to remember where she knew the little guy from. She hoped and prayed he wasn't someone she had given her illness to. She didn't think so because he didn't sound angry when he called her.

"Oh my God, am I glad I found you. Misty, I need your help. I'm lost." he told her all out of breath.

Recollection finally made it to her mind. It was the little guy from the motel. "Oh hi! I haven't seen you round the spot since the raid. Are you okay?" she asked him, thinking in her mind that this could be a come up for her.

"Naaw. I'm not alright, Misty. I'm lost. The night of the raid I jumped out of the bathroom window and ran. I ran so fucking far that by the time I realized it. I didn't know where I was. I can't find my way back over to the spot with Chill Will." He was rambling trying to get it all out at once.

"Oh, that's easy sugar, it's just a few blocks up the street from here. But Chill Will's not there anymore honey. Him and Miriam pulled up and left last night."

Lolo couldn't believe it. He came so close by some miracle he'd found his way back only to be too late.

He couldn't take it any longer. He just plopped down right on the sidewalk. He was utterly defeated!

"No, no, no, no, no." he just kept repeating to himself.

"What's the matter, sugar?" She looked around nervously Lolo hadn't realized the .38 fell out of his pocket.

"He had everything. What am I gone do now." he was sitting there talking to himself, but she answered him anyway.

"Aww sugar, you don't think Chill Will hustled you, do you?"

Lolo didn't know what to say. Hell, he couldn't talk. He wanted to scream, wanted to cry, and wanted to kill somebody all at the same time.

"You know sugar, he did wait around for two days. But the spot had gotten hot since that night. The damn deputies kept driving by, making everybody all nervous honey. Shit, with as much work as you guys had, I'm surprised he waited around as long as he did." If what she was saying was true maybe that's what happened. Maybe Chill Will got too nervous to stay sitting at that motel with all that product because of the deputies.

Rationalizing the situation, he realized that it really didn't matter why Chill Will left. What was important was figuring out how was Lolo going to find him now.

"Sugar, you mean to tell me, all that money you guys were making, and you didn't put any of it up! Or stash it somewhere?"

Lolo didn't even have the energy to answer her. Clearly the drugs must've fried her brain cells for her to be asking him such dumb ass questions. Yeah, he stashed his money. He just stashed it in the wrong damn place.

"I'll tell you what sugar. If you want, you can rest up a while at my place. You look a little tired. Who knows, once you rest up a spell, you might think of something or remember something that may help you find out where he went. Who knows, I may even suck your cock and make you feel better." If Lolo had any food in his stomach, he surely would've thrown it up. All of it. There was no way in hell he would let her put her nasty ass stank breath mouth on him. Lolo didn't care how good it would make him feel.

However, sitting down, relaxing, and resting for a minute would surely do him some good. He'd been walking nonstop since he escaped out of the room.

"Make sure you tuck your gun somewhere more secure this time." she told Lolo as he got to his feet.

Neither of them paid any attention to the people they passed by who stared at the white streetwalker and the little black boy. Who

157

were walking down the street together. Each lost in their own thoughts, mired in their own separate world.

It only took about ten minutes or so to walk to Misty's place. She just happened to stay around the corner from the Capri Motel.

When they got there, Lolo didn't know what the fuck was going on. If there was a God, surely Lolo must've pissed him off in the previous life or something. Because every time he thought he caught a break, things just seemed to get worse.

Misty's place looked worse than the abandoned house that he and Nyomi stayed at in East Palo Alto. Trash and bullshit was piled literally two and a half feet high. Shit stacked on top of shit all throughout. Lolo couldn't see a clear or clean spot anywhere he looked. Which was no surprise because Misty hadn't seen her carpet in two years.

"I know it's a little messy but make yourself at home and get comfortable." she said this like it was only one or two dishes laying around.

The smell was unlike anything he had ever encountered before. Misty climbed over a giant pile of trash, and with one arm she swept a portion of it onto the pile of garbage covering what had to be the ground.

Once that was done. Lolo was able to make out what appeared to be a broken-down, worn-out couch. Misty patted the spot next to her.

"Come on now sugar. Take a seat, ol' Misty don't bite." When she smiled her teeth were stained brown and yellow.

Lolo climbed his way over to the couch and sat on the spot she putted for him. He couldn't quite get comfortable. So, he put his hands on the couch cushion to adjust himself. His right hand landed on something cold, slimy, and wet. He was afraid to look down and see what he touched.

When he finally did gain the courage to look down to see just what his hand landed in, he wanted to scream. His hand landed on a used old condom. The slimy wet stuff that he touched was the semen spilling out of the condom.

Misty was oblivious to all of this. Her concentration was focused on the long stem full of crack that was in her lips.

Lolo shuddered; he shook as much of the semen off his fingers as he could before vigorously rubbing his hands on his pants.

"Here sugar, try this, maybe it will make you feel better.

It always takes Mama's pain away." Misty offered him the crack pipe. After all the shit he'd been through, Lolo figured why not? Life just wouldn't stop fucking with him. Something that would ease this pain was just what the doctor ordered.

Lolo grabbed the stem and lighter out of her hands. The burnt, sweet, pungent smell of the crack was ten times better than the smell inside her place.

"Let it take all your pain away, sugar." Her voice sounded so seductive as she coached him forward to smoking the crack.

He put the stem to his lips. Then he had an epiphany. Is this how he wanted to end up? Was he okay with becoming a meaningless, crack-head homeless on the streets? Roaming and rummaging any and everywhere he could for food or shelter. Going days or even months without washing his ass.

He lit the lighter and brought it up to the stem.

"Do you wanna die the same way T'Rida did?" He heard the soft voice but didn't know where it came from.

"Son, you're better than this, you're better than I was. Inside of you is all of me. My strengths and my weaknesses. Navigate to my strengths. Don't let yourself migrate to the weaknesses. Be better than that. The voice of his father T'Rida whispered in his ear.

Suddenly a pile of trash over in the corner moved, scaring the fuck out of him. He didn't stay long enough to find out what it was.

159

"Man, fuck this shit!" He called out, tossing the crack stem and lighters, and getting the fuck up out of there.

The last image he had of Misty who screamed out when he tossed the stem was of her searching wildly through the piles of trash on the floor for the crack stem.

Leaving out of Misty's Personal Purgatory, Lolo realized two things. The first being that he had to go all the way back to the beginning in order to be able to correct his current situation and position in life.

Second, he knew the spirits of his father and mother were always with him. They would be with him to help guide him through the fucked-up maze of life.

He wound up finding his way back around to the Capri Motel only to learn that Misty had been telling the truth. Any and all signs of Chill Will and Miriam were long gone.

Instead of wallowing in self-pity and a bunch of self-destructive thoughts. Lolo decided to head out on the long, long trek back to East Menlo Park and East Palo Alto. He had to get up out of Redwood City.

With that in mind, he set out on his journey walking down Whipple Road heading for Veterans Blvd.

Roughly four blocks away from the Capri the weight of the gun inside his pocket began irritating him. He grabbed the .38 and prepared to toss it when all of a sudden, an idea came to him.

On the next corner he could see a gas station and with a smile on his face he raced across the street heading for the gas station. There was a young nigga driving a black and red Chevy Camaro over by the water and air station. This is where Lolo headed.

"Say my man! Can I ask you question?" Lolo called out as he approached the nigga who was putting air in his tires.

160

The nigga looked up, for a moment then went back to paying attention to what he was doing.

"What's up youngsta?" he called over his shoulder not paying too much attention to the little kid that came up to him.

"If you had the choice would you rather give me a ride to Menlo Park or have me take yo shit?" Lolo said this in a nonchalant voice.

The guy filling his tire with air chuckled. "That's a hellavah question to ask somebody, little man."

"Yeah, but it's a serious question, so answer it." This time the guy could detect the underlying threat.

When he filled the tire with air and stood up, he noticed the gun clutched in the kid's hand. Now he may have been a kid, but DJ could tell it was a real gun. Which made matters worse, because if the kid didn't fully appreciate the danger of a gun, DJ could be fucked.

Quickly assessing the situation, DJ looked the kid over from his dirty wrinkled clothes to the tiredness he saw in the kid's eyes. He was looking at someone with nothing to lose. The proof of which was in the fact that he was ready to car jack DJ in broad daylight.

The wrinkled pants the kid had on were True Religion Jeans that cost about $200 a pair. So, whatever the kid's story, he wasn't always in a I don't give a fuck scenario.

More proof was in the fact that he couldn't smell the "danger" he put himself in. DJ stood about 5'11" looked to weigh maybe 180 lbs. He was light skinned with a warm smile. However, his eyes told a story of murder and violence. A story that Lolo couldn't read.

"I'll tell you what lil Homie. Put that banger away before you draw the wrong kind of attention to us. And I'll give you a ride to Menlo. I'm actually headed that way anyway." A part of DJ related to the lil Homie. The other part understood where he was at mentally. Because DJ had been there before himself, years ago.

"And you have to buy me some food too!" Lolo threw in there after looking at the iced-out dragon chain that DJ wore around his neck.

Lolo guessed the guy had to be balling to be able to afford a neck- lace like that, with all the diamonds glittering all over it.

Hearing this DJ actually laughed out loud. He could hear the plea of desperation inside of the kid's voice.

"Damn lil nigga, you're just full of demands ain't you!" DJ smiled and shook his head. "Come on, jump in."

As DJ walked back around to the driver's side of his car Lolo climbed into the passenger side. Once DJ got into the car, he stared at the little nigga so long it made Lolo uncomfortable.

"Say Homie. I ain't wit none of the weirdo shit. I just need something to eat and a ride to Menlo. I'm lost, tired and haven't eaten in three days." Lolo honestly told him.

"Well, that's good lil Homie. Cause I definitely ain't wit none of the weirdo shit." DJ told him as he shook his head in amazement. Then, started the car.

There was something about the little nigga, but DJ just couldn't put his finger on what it was. He wished he could place it, but he just couldn't. Time was money so he said, "Fuck it, let's go." and pulled off.

He pulled up into In and Out Burger off of Veterans Blvd and ordered two, two-by-two's both animal style!

"What's yo name, lil Homie?" DJ asked him once the food came and he handed the kid his food.

Lolo tore into the food like a wild animal!

"Thomas, but they call me Lolo." he mumbled with a mountain of food in his mouth.

"Goddamn." That's it, DJ thought to himself. It was an eerie feeling, but the kid reminded him so much of his fallen

162

leader, T'Rida, in his mannerisms. He was a spitting image of T'Rida's son, Titas. Could it have been possible for T'Rida to have other children? Naw, somebody in the family would have known about it.

Lost in thought, DJ drove off while Lolo went to work on his second burger and fries. Kendrick Lamar spit fire through the speakers as they made their way down Highway 101, headed for Menlo Park.

A call came over his phone. The digital computer screen in the dash read Keak. His brother.

"What up Keak?" he answered once he hit the button on the steering wheel.

"D, where you at nigga? We over here everybody is waiting on you." Keak's voice came over the car speakers.

He was at the War Room along with everyone else waiting on DJ to start the meeting.

"Brah, I'm like fifteen away. I had to fix a slow leak in one of my tires and get some air." DJ answered back.

"I'll let everybody know. Hurry up though." Keak hung up the phone without waiting for reply and Kendrick came back to life in the speakers.

A few minutes later he was taking the Willow Road exit.

"Where you want me to take you?" he asked Lolo as they pulled up to a stop light.

"This good right here. Thanks, big Homie." Lolo shouted as he bolted out the car and took off down Bay Rd. heading towards Midtown, East Palo Alto.

DJ started to turn the Camaro in that direction and go after him, but the Mobb was waiting. He had a meeting to attend.

CHAPTER NINETEEN

For almost a week now he's been roaming the streets of East Palo Alto doing any and everything one could imagine to survive. From sleeping inside of broken-down abandoned cars to stealing food out of all the Mexican bodegas in the area.

At one point, Lolo wondered how this could be the hood, and yet not one store he has come across have been black owned. Every store he walked in was owned by fucking Mexicans. It was not like that down in Stockton and Tracy where he lived with Mama Jennifer. In Stockton, you saw Black owned liquor stores. What could've happened to the city he wondered for it to have been overrun by Mexicans?

He was on his way to his new hiding place. A storage room inside of a small apartment complex on Cooley Avenue. The complex itself seemed to have all Mexicans or at least a majority Mexicans living there. The night he first entered the complex he was going to break into a couple of cars. The first car he checked out was unlocked, but the moment he opened the door he heard voices of a couple of people heading his way. There was a door to a storage room behind him. He quickly checked the handle; the door was locked yet when he pushed a little it opened. Lolo quickly ducked inside of the storage room.

It was a good thing because the three dudes that were coming got into the Impala that he was about to go in. By the looks of the three of them they would've really roughed him up if they would've caught him inside the car.

Making things even sweeter was there was a small window at the back of the storage container. The window looked like it hadn't been used in almost a decade. He found a way to leave it jimmied in case he ever came back, and the door was locked in a way he could not get it open.

He only used the storage closet on one other time since that night. He figured if he came too frequently the chance would be greater of someone finding out about him staying in the closet.

Using this logic, he made it a habit not to stay in the same place two nights in a row if he did not have to. He had a few different places throughout the city to lay his head. Some were more comfort- able than the others.

However, they all served their purpose.

A little way up the block he spotted someone walking towards him. From the way they were walking they were barely able to stay on their feet. As he got closer, Lolo realized it was a drunk Paisa, the sun had just gone down probably an hour ago. But seeing a drunk Mexican in East Palo Alto at any time of the day was not unusual.

The Paisa was actually about Lolo's size and height. He was a lot heavier than Lolo, but they were the same height, Lolo quickly scanned the area. He didn't see anyone else out on the street or any nosy neighbors looking out of their windows.

Lolo reached inside of his hooded sweater and pulled out the .38. Timing is everything, Lolo slowed down enough so that by the time he and the drunk met up with each other, it would be on the side of the old camper that was parked on their side of the street. When they passed each other, the drunk did not even acknowledge Lolo's presence. Lolo quickly spins around and at the same time his hand shoots up and he cracks the drunk in the back of the head with the butt of the gun.

The Paisa dropped to the ground like a 50 lbs. sack of potatoes. Lights out, snoring before he reached the ground. Lolo goes through his pants pockets, socks, and the pocket of his drawers in under twenty seconds. Stuffing the wad of cash, he found in the drawers and his left pants pocket into his own pockets. Ten seconds later Lolo has the black leather jacket off his victim and on his body, walking away.

He glanced backwards one last time to make sure no one was sneaking up on him. The drunk Paisa lays helplessly on his back with his pockets turned inside out. His pants unbuckled and pulled halfway down. One man's loss is simply another's gain.

Going to the storage room is now out of the question.

Lolo quickly turns right on Runnymede and left on Capitol. After going a block, he turns right on Bell St. crosses the light and disappears into the shadows at Bell Street Park.

He walks behind the bushes to another tuck spot that he has. There's a 3 ½ foot gap that separates the back of the bushes from the gate that separates the park from Drew Medical Center. Finding his favorite spot up under an oak tree, Lolo takes a seat and pulls out everything that he took from the drunk Paisa.

Out of everything he took, the first thing to catch his attention is an open pack of Big Red chewing gum. He opens two sticks of gum and placed them in his mouth. Next, he sees an antique Zippo lighter that has some ancient Aztec shit engraved on it, then a pack of breath mints, $3.77 in change, a lottery ticket, a receipt from 76 gas station and some dollar bills.

The lottery ticket, breath mints, lighter and change goes back into his pocket. A couple of dope fiends just happened to be passing at the exact moment the change makes noise. One of the dope friends stops and calls out. "Hey, whatcha got going on back there?"

"A bullet in yo ass if you come behind these bushes to find out." Lolo already pulled the gun out and had it pointed in the direction the voice came from.

The dope fiend stops and ponders if it's really worth finding out until his partner grabs him by his shoulders.

"Man, come on fool and stop fucking with people before you mess around and get us shot!" He's clearly afraid plus he wants to hurry up and get to the benches and smoke his dope.

Reluctantly the first dope fiend takes his partner's advice and moves along, but his nosiness can't allow him to do anything else but wonder what the guy was doing behind the bushes. Plus, the voice sounded a little too soft to be taken seriously. Like the voice of a teenager. Lolo kept the gun pointed towards the direction they were walking. The second dope fiend was fussing all the way until they were out of earshot.

When he could no longer hear them, Lolo puts the gun back on his lap and begins sorting the cash bills that he took from the Mexican. Once he's done putting it together, he counts it $403.00. This pleases Lolo, not only did he get a new black leather jacket, but he also has enough to eat for almost a month.

It's too late to get some real food unless he wanted to walk all the way to McDonald's which he didn't feel like doing. Lolo decides to just wait long enough for the dope fiends to leave. When they do, he would walk over to the dumpsters at Elysian Fields, which are at the front side of the park. That's where he will sleep tonight.

Somehow though while waiting he dozes off with the gun sitting right on his lap.

A little while later something wakes him up. Still groggy from the sleep he reaches for the gun but it's not on his lap. He uses his hands to see if he could feel it, but he doesn't.

"Unh huh. What are you looking for? you lil piece of shit?" Lolo was now alarmed. It's the dope fiend from earlier. Somehow, he has managed to sneak behind the bushes and grab the gun off of Lolo's lap without him knowing.

"You know I thought you was bullshitting about hitting a nigga with some hot shit bullets. But I's see you was a fa'sho serious, little nigga." It was too dark now for Lolo to be able to see his face on this moonless night. But he could see the guy standing right over him.

"So now I figure if a little muthafucka has a gun. He must be either getting ready to take some shit. Or he already done took some shit.

"Now wit you being all back here hiding out and shit, I's think you done already took some shit. What you think?" When he smiled Lolo was able to see his butter yellow teeth.

"Man, look I'm sitting over here minding my own business just trying to get some sleep. Why don't you just gone and give me my shit back and go-on about your business." Lolo really wasn't in the mood for no bullshit.

"Ain't dis about a bitch! How's I'm the one with the gun but you're still talking shit?" The dope fiend really found humor in that.

"How's about I go on about my business?" he mimicked shockingly.

"How about…. I tell you what. How's about you break yo muthafuck'n self nigga!" The dope fiend began bouncing up and down hyped up.

"W-what?"

"Break yo'self bitch! Come on, come on, come on, and empty dem muthafuck'n pockets! Boo Boo!" While he was bouncing in the air his arm was stretched out with his palm open tapping upwards like he had an invisible Ping-Pong paddle.

Lolo had no choice but to turn out his pockets and hand over the money.

"Fucking faggot ass dope fiend." He mumbled as he handed the money over.

"Watch your mouth nigga before it really get ugly up in this bitch, Boo Boo! Oh yes, we getting high tonight." The happier he got the more he acted like a female.

"That's it! You can get your faggot ass outta here."

"Ooh, uh-uh. Call me one more faggot, bitch and I'll show you a faggot." Now he sounded manly. Now that his feelings were hurt.

168

"Faggot ass nigga!" Lolo didn't know where the anger was coming from and all the hatred, because he didn't have anything against homosexuals.

"Okay bitch! Now Mama's got to teach him." Lolo realized maybe he fucked up because the dope fiend was unbuckling his pants.

"Now you gonna suck Mama's dick so she can show you who the faggot is, bitch!" The nigga was fuming now. "O-Okay. Okay man, my bad I wasn't trying to disrespect you, I was just pissed off." Lolo tried to defuse the situation. The level of fear that he felt at that present moment was indescribable.

The dope fiend's eyes jumped around so erratically inside of his head that Lolo realized now a little too late that he doesn't have it all together. He was so high that he was having trouble undoing his pants and was practically foaming at the mouth.

"You already got the money, folks just let me leave." Lolo tried to get up, but when he did, the dope fiend punches him hard in the face.

He finally freed his flaccid penis and wiggled it at Lolo. "Come on bitch, suck Mama's cock." he taunted.

"No!"

Lolo shook his head side to side franticly as tears streamed down his cheeks.

The dope fiend strikes him in the face again. This time Lolo loss his hearing for a moment and grew dizzy.

Another blow to the head like that and he'll knock Lolo out. A fear greater than he has ever experienced engulfs Lolo. There's no telling what the dope fiend will do to him if he's unconscious and Lolo knows this.

"Okay! Okay!" He finally concedes. Anything to stop the blows from raining down on him.

Yeah that's right. Come on bitch!" The dope fiend smiles again sadistically as he steps closer to Lolo.

The hand with the gun in it rests down by his side with his free hand he grabs Lolo by the back of his head forcing his head closer to his penis.

Lolo knows what he must do, and it sickens him. But it is his only option, he has no other choice. He opens his mouth which has become bone dry from fear.

"Yeah that's right, come on." The dope fiend mumbles as he feels himself entering Lolo's mouth. "Damn that shit feels good."

Lolo wants to throw up but knows he can't if he wants to live, he must do it. The dope fiend's penis was about halfway in Lolo's mouth now.

"Now!" Lolo screams to himself inside of his head. "AAAaaaarrrrgh!" The scream pierces through the night like an

arrow launched from a mighty hunter.

The dope fiend collapses right there a foot in front of Lolo in agony and grief. He continues to scream like the little bitch that he is. Rolling around on the ground, grabbing himself.

The copper taste of blood fills Lolo's mouth. The look in his eyes is manic.

"Psstewww" he spits out the chunk of the dope fiend's penis that he bit off out his mouth.

Now it's Lolo's turn to do the taunting! "Aaw, what's the matter? Did you hurt your little wee-wee?" Saliva and blood run down his chin, adding to his crazed look and he's panting like a wild animal.

Lolo retrieves the gun that the dope fiend dropped when he bit his dick off.

"You thought you was going to try and homo me?" Lolo yells in rage as he starts shooting.

"Huh bitch? Now what you gonna do?" "You faggot fuck!"

All six bullets find their mark. The first two zeroed in on his head while the rest made mincemeat out of his chest cavity. To add insult to injury, Lolo walked over and kicked him in the head.

He didn't panic he calmly reached into the dope fiend's pocket and retrieved his money before walking away.

Melting into the shadows once again.

CHAPTER TWENTY

After scalding Terrence with the boiling water, Dirt went back upstairs and slept on the sofa in the living room. The next morning, he woke up feeling more rested than he had in a long, long time. The last time he slept so well was the last night at the Capri Motel with Nyomi. So much has happened since then that it feels like that was a lifetime ago.

There hasn't been a day that has gone by that he didn't think about her. Though the time that they spent with each other was relatively short, their bond was as strong as any bond could form.

That morning, Dirt decided to do a more thorough search of the house to see what he could come up with. The two most interesting things were Terrence didn't have any other family or friends.

Some bank papers that he found told him that Terrence lived off some old trust account. No job, family, or friends meant no one would come looking for ol' Terrence. Dirt also found that the house was as secure as the U.S. Mint. There were cameras all throughout the house as well as outside of the house.

Every monitor could be viewed from Terrence's room. Motion detectors with video were in the front and back yard and attached to the gates. Inside of Terrence's closet was a safe with a key. Dirt found the key on the key ring he removed from off of Terrence's body. The safe held a little cash, a pearl handled 45, some old coins and a black book. Also, inside of the closet were a few more guns and some weird looking knives. Two hours after he began his search Dirt was done and he was hungry.

Using the back door like Terrence used, he came around to the front yard from the side of the house. He walked to the taco spot on Willow Road. thinking about his next move. After placing his order of four Carne Asada tacos with cheese and sour cream and one Super Burrito. Dirt decided to eat there instead of taking the food to go, he'd been cooped up in that house forever.

Someone left a newspaper on the table, Dirt decided to pick it up and see what he could learn. Looking at the date Dirt realized that it was February 11th, his birthday.

A smile appeared on his face.

"Would you look at that, today is the kid's birthday." He spoke out loud to no one in particular.

When his food came, the woman that brought it to him looked very familiar, but he did not know why. Pouring some hot sauce on his tacos, the Carne Asada had his stomach doing back flips it smelled so good. As hungry as he was, Dirt refused to devour the food. Today was his day, so he was going to take his time and enjoy it!

The food was a wonderful present from himself to himself, as was his freedom. He was free! A nigga could not really ask for more than that. If today was his birthday, then that meant Terrence held him hostage for almost nine months Dirt could not believe that shit.

After polishing off his plate, he ordered another Super Burrito to go. That's when the recollection hit him about the woman. She was the woman from the picture. The wife of the guy that was trying to have her killed. Dirt wondered how that ended up working out. The woman saw the little boy starring at her and smiled, she was beautiful.

Back at the house, Dirt still hadn't come up with a plan of action yet. He no longer had to worry about where he would sleep for the night. Terrence's house would become his house.

Now hopes of finding Nyomi was all that was on his mind. That and teaching Terrence's sick ass a lesson. First, he was going to see what he could do about getting some information on Nyomi.

During his search of Terrence's room, he found two laptops. Back in the living room Dirt searched the web for anything he could find, which wasn't much. Halfway through the search he realized he wasn't going to be able to find

174

anything out, but he refused to give up. When it came to finding information on juveniles everybody and everything was zipped shut.

Over an hour into his search, he came across an article in the Daily Journal Newspaper that got his attention. The article said an anonymous caller called 911 to report a man suspected of lewd acts with a minor.

When Sherriff's deputies arrived on the scene, they found a teenage girl in a room with a large amount of cocaine in her possession. Deputies report that when they gained access into the room. The girl was found trying to flee through a window in the bathroom.

The drugs were found to be in her possession at the time of the incident. A concerned citizen who spoke to deputies reported seeing someone flee out of the window in question and disappear down the alley. The concerned citizen wanted to remain anonymous.

Spokesperson for the Sheriff's Department did confirm the arrest following the lead from the tipster. However, quoted that was all that could be shared, citing an ongoing investigation the name of the young girl was held.

The Sheriff's spokesperson would like anyone with any information involving the matter to call 1-800-Crime Stoppers. You could leave information anonymously.

After reading the article Dirt was pissed. All this time he thought the raid had something to do with the rapist they killed in that abandoned house.

The article for sure was about them. There was no question about that. Yet the article clearly said someone called in with a tip.

For a long time, Dirt sat starring at the screen wondering. He was trying to think who could have called in a tip on them, everyone loved Chill Will because from what they'd seen he was one of them and he was making it. Somehow it gave them all hope that they themselves could one day get their shit together.

Plus, both Chill Will and Lolo treated each and every customer with respect and dignity. Never once trying to stunt on them or put them down.

He was thinking so hard that his head began to hurt. Dirt decided to let the topic drop for a while vowing that he would return to it later.

That's when it happened. The memory knocked him upside the head like a blow from James Ward. The only person they had gotten into it with was the bitch ass child molester, Von Jack.

Dirt remembered how he had to get out of the shower because of the loud commotion he was causing. Von Jack even tried to flex on him. It wasn't until he seen his little buddy clutched in Dirt's hand that the nigga decided to act like he had some get right.

"Muthafucka!" without thinking, Dirt slammed his fist into the screen of the notebook.

The punk ass pedophile was the reason he was separated from the love of his life. He couldn't bear to come at a ten-year- old boy on-some gangsta shit! Instead, the maggot piece of shit put salt in the game by calling them people.

That's okay! He will make sure that along with Terrence, he would teach Von a valuable lesson as well.

But first he had to find him. The only things that Dirt knew about Von was that he sold drugs, he was from East Palo Alto, and he liked little girls. Right at that moment, the one thing that was good enough to give Dirt some hope of finding him was the fact that he was in East Palo Alto. The same place that Von was from.

Dirt would have to find a way to blend in, join the ranks, and take over the street life in East Palo Alto if he wanted to have any success in catching up to Von.

Right now, anybody looking at him would only see a kid. No one would take him seriously. First things first, he would have to get people to start recognizing him. Once they recognized him, he would make them respect him.

One thing that he learned from Chill Will was, in the streets respect was everything. You either had it or you did not. Fear and love were the other equal sides to that pyramid of the game.

Of all the niggaz who became successful in the game, they had conquered and mastered one side of the pyramid. They were either loved and respected or feared.

Rarely did someone come to rise through the ranks that welded all three sides of the spectrum. That person was beyond greatness. He was the epitome of a gangsta!

Someone like New York's own Black Caesar, Frank Mathews.

A Black man who told the Italian Mafia at the height of their reign to suck his black dick when they tried to make him pay taxes for selling dope in what they felt was their state.

Respected so much by his people that he had an army of brothas, some say a thousand strong across twenty-one states, they had his back. Feared so much that even Philly's own Black Mafia had to bow down to his gangsta when war began brewing. All because they too, tried to strong-arm Black Caesar. Loved and idolized so much, Hollywood made movies about him starring Pam Grier. Musicians named their bands after him, like The Frank Mathews Band.

Becoming respected, feared, or loved in an organization so large one thing was true, every member remained loyal. Not one person ever turned state's witness or snitched on him.

Another name that Chill Will liked to speak on, was Washington D.C.'s own Michael Frey. The older cousin of the highly feared, respected, loved, and infamous Wayne Perry. Wayne Perry was so respected and feared. His case was the first ever in history where the feds offered the kingpin a deal if he snitched on his enforcer, which Alfonso "Alpo" Ramirez did. Alpo snitched on the very man that protected and worked for him.

From what Chill Will told Dirt about Michael Frey, he was in a league all his own. One of the few legendary street figures that was not a kingpin or leader of an organization. Michael Frey Salters was truly a one-man army. He walked alone in prison yards where other killers walked in groups. He was the first man to ever be accepted freely in every part of the murderous Washington D.C streets. The only person in history ever, to be paid one million dollars to squash a beef between two warring factions. All he did was mediate.

Dirt was going to take the stories taught to him by Chilly Willy and use them as a blueprint to follow. Within those stories were the do's and the don'ts to becoming who, or what, he needed to become in order for him to take over the underworld.

He knew that first he needed to become a Predator in order for the street to fear him. Then he must become a Hood-Star for the same streets to love and respect him. He and his Queen, because he would find Nyomi, his true love no matter what it took! No matter what he had to do or where he had to go.

First things first... what to do about Terrence?

CHAPTER TWENTY ONE

*Lolo was outraged! Fucking faggot junkie. "Pstwet!"
No matter how many times he spit, he couldn't get the coppery
taste of blood out of his mouth.*

*The moment the dope-fiend forced himself inside of
Lolo's mouth, something inside of his mind and soul snapped.*

*Never again will he allow himself to be victimized or
put in the position where he felt he was the "victim." Whatever
it took, what- ever it called for, whatever the consequences, he
would always be the "victor!"*

*"Hey, you. What are you doing over there?" the
question brought Lolo out if his trance and back to reality.*

*From the way the voice sounded he knew it had to be a
cop. He couldn't stop, couldn't turn around. If he
acknowledged the cop, he would have to engage in a
conversation with him. He cop would no doubt wonder what a
kid was doing out on the streets at this time a night.*

*He would want to ask all kinds of questions and would
search Lolo. Where he would find the gun that had already
killed two people.*

*Lolo was less than three feet from the corner of Bell
Street and Euclid Avenue. The cop sounded at least twenty feet
back, Lolo kept walking like he hadn't heard the question as he
turned the corner. He cut his eyes to the left and seen that he
was right. The cop was halfway down the street. As soon as he
was out of visual range Lolo bolted!*

*Instead of going down the street like most people would
have. Lolo bolted across the street and jumped the gate into the
back yard. He was over the gate and in the backyard before the
cop even reached the corner. Unfortunately, it was a Mexican
house with a chicken coop. Startled by his presence, the
chickens and roosters started going crazy. Lolo dashed across*

the yard. Something emerged from the shadows charging towards him.

He was too scared to even consider what it could be. In a panic he lunged for the gate leading to the other yard just as the jaws of a Doberman Pincher snapped at his heels. Lolo landed on his back in the other yard knocking his wind out. He could not let the pain stop him.

"Goddamn it, I said freeze! Whoa... Shiiit!" the Doberman would keep that officer busy for a while. Hopping the next gate brought him out on Oakwood Drive. Lolo's chest felt like he'd swallowed a simmering hot coal. He could hear sirens close by but could not stop to wonder where they were. He sprinted across the street. As soon as he reached the big oak tree in the middle of the street, a squad car zipped by.

"Scuuurrr!" He must've seen Lolo because he hit the brakes immediately then threw the car into reverse. Filling the street up with smoke and the smell of burnt rubber.

Lolo took off like a Bat out of Hell down Oakwood Street, heading straight towards Bay Road. He dipped between a painter's van and a construction truck. He knew his best bet was hitting gates. He wouldn't be able to outrun the police car. So, he took to the gates. Not only was he hitting gates, but he was going in a sporadic pattern.

Before he knew it, he came out on the street St. John's Church was on. Out of the blue it began raining. Not no little drizzle rain either. It was full on storming. Like the old folks used to say, "It was raining cats and dogs."

Visibility just went from a half a mile down the road to not even halfway down the block, Lolo knew this would help him. He sprinted as fast as he could and jumped the gate to St. John's Church. This was his destination, and he was hellbent on making it there!

His legs felt like cinderblocks were attached to his feet, but he pushed with all he had. Striking across the open parking lot he thought he wasn't going to make it, but he finally did.

Only to find out that they placed a padlock on the dumpster. It wasn't looking wasn't looking too good. His only options were to hide

181

by the dumpster and hope that he would go unnoticed, or to take his chances and keep on trekking. He chose the latter.

Waiting by the dumpster he was a sitting duck and he wasn't going out like that; He ran toward the building and hid inside its shadows. Two squad cars sped by right in front of his face. Lolo's only thoughts were he was in a race for his life and being hunted for murder.

The second dope fiend had stopped one of the police cars and reported his lover's murder, after stumbling over his body in the park. As soon as the two cars turned the corner, he made his move.

Lucky for him the main point of focus for the police was around the Oakwood area. One of the officers thought they saw him double back toward University Avenue.

Coming down Laurel Avenue a set of headlights turning onto the street from Bay Road made him jump another gate and come out on the 1100 block of Jervis Avenue. Lolo wasn't going to chance running down Bay Road considering it was a main street through town.

He crossed the street and kept going until he reached Alberni Street. The street was so dark that he was able to rest for a moment. Plus, he'd covered considerable distance from Elysian Fields and Bell St. Park. Yet he still had to cut across the six-lane highway that was Willow Road.

Willow Road was the busiest street in Menlo Park. It was too dark to be able to make out police headlights. He couldn't afford to jump out of the darkness at the wrong time. Lolo waited for the next break in traffic and took his chances.

He made it across safely without seeing any red and blue lights. Finally, he found a dumpster behind the taco shack. Feeling victorious and being tired, cold, wet, hungry and bunch of other things he climbed into the dumpster hoping he would find some rest.

His plans of sleeping in the dumpster ended when the rain began seeping in from the cracks in the rubber lid. He had to leave. If he had stayed, maybe his life would've gone down a different path.

CHAPTER TWENTY TWO

Dirt had a game plan now and was going to see it through to the end. First, he had to backtrack. He had to return to the abandoned house where he met Nyomi.

Stepping into the house brought back memories of his lost love. The memories made him smile at first before the frown came. The memories were bittersweet. At one point he had to bite his bottom lip to keep himself from dropping a tear.

Keeping to his task he muscled through the memories and garbage alike. When he got to the back room, he didn't try to prepare himself for what he was going to see. He didn't give a fuck!

Looking at the bones of the first person he had ever killed, Dirt wished he still had bullets in his gun. He would shoot the muthafucka again. Instead, he hawked up a big loogey and spit on the bones. The slimy goo landed right inside of the skeleton's right eye.

"No respect for the dead I see!" Hearing this, Lolo spun around, upset that someone had snuck up on him.

"Fuck him! And what's it to you?" he challenged with an angry mug on his face.

"Well now, the O.G. don't really give two fucks about him." The intruder spoke in a familiar voice.

"Chill Will! Goddamn man, I thought..." Dirt couldn't bring himself to complete the sentence and let his idol know the disrespectful things that ran through his hand.

"Sheeeiiit it's okay, lil Homie. If a dope fiend, I had just met had my total life's saving and disappeared, I'd probably think some negative shit too." Chill Will tried to make him feel better. "Shit, big Homie I'm glad to see you." Dirt couldn't contain his excitement.

Sure, he'd gained a little weight. His clothes looked brand new. But it was Chill Will. The biggest difference that Dirt could see as he stared in disbelief was the glow.

Dirt didn't know what it was or why it was there, but Chill Will had a glow about him that made him look newer than his clothes. Dirt couldn't have known it was the glow of a man who got his swagger back.

"Come on, let's get up out of here and the O.G. will catch you up to speed." There was even a sparkle in Chill Will's eyes.

"Fa'sho, big Homie!" The two turned to leave.

Then Dirt remembered why he'd came there to begin with. "Hold up real quick, big Homie."

Dirt scrounged around for a couple of minutes while he searched for what he'd come for. Finally, he found it under a pile of rubbish. He snatched it up, then walked towards Chill Will.

"Alright big Homie, I'm straight." Side-by-side, Chill Will, and Dirt emerged from the abandoned building.

Two niggaz that look like they emerged straight off of New Jack City were posted out front. For the second time in just ten minutes Dirt wished he had some bullets.

"Everything straight, Boss?" The scariest of the two asked.

Dirt looked at Chill Will like he had a mound of dog shit on top of his head.

"Boss?" he asked with a puzzled look.

Chill Will chuckled. Then turned his attention to the nigga that asked the question.

"Yeah Dave, we good Homie." Chill told his vicious attack dog.

Dave looked over to his brother, Poppa. They spoke a silent language just by looking at each other. The shit still was creepy to Chill Will.

Dave led the group of four with Poppa picking up the rear. Across the street shining like it was still wet, was a brand new black-on-black tinted Cadillac Escalade. The four men made their way over to the Escalade.

Dirt was speechless! A huge smile came across his face. He was so proud of his big Homie that he was stunned. It wasn't every day that someone witnessed a real-life comeback story. Let alone to have actually been a part of one. A lot of comeback stories never fully make it back. Once the getting was getting good, they'd fall off and start fucking up again. Not Chill Will. For years he'd been waiting to get back in the game. Now that he'd gotten his chance. He was going for league M.V.P.

Poppa and Dave climbed into the front, while Chill Will and Dirt climbed into the back. This wasn't an urban novel. Niggaz opened their own muthafuck'n doors around here.

Once they pulled off Chill Will began talking. "Shyeeeiit lil Homie, the O.G. almost wrote you off and stopped coming to that old house. I went to that house and sat in my truck for two hours in the daytime and two hours at night just waiting for you to show up....

"But how did you?" Dirt interrupted.

"Wait just a minute, now. I'm getting to that." Chill Will pulled out a fat Cuban cigar and stuck it between his teeth savoring the taste, then he continued.

"You see when you were sharing with me some of the things you had been through that led to ya'll being at the Capri Motel. The O.G. paid good attention because there is something special about you lil Homie. Now I can't quite say what it is, but I see it."

"I could tell by the way y'all carried yourselves that you two were good kids. Yet I could also tell that y'all was running from something by the way you moved and kept your head on a swivel."

"Now I told you that I used to be in the game heavily. Well, what I didn't tell you was East Palo Alto was my stomping grounds. I came up under the Dust Man Era. And I still remembered the area. So, when you described the area where you and Nyomi stayed at, I knew it

187

had to be in the Gardens, area." Chill Will paused and lit his cigar and inhaled deeply. Dirt waited patiently and respectfully for him to finish.

"I waited around at the Capri for a couple of days, but it got too hot to be there. Vice kept showing up and they dirty asses don't play. All I could do was wait on you to come to me."

"But how did you know this was the right house?" Dirt was lost.

"Sheeiit, that muthafucka back there told me." he laughed at his own joke. "When I came through there were only two abandoned houses in the Gardens. One was on Azalia Drive, and that one back there. I checked them both out. Crackheads overran the one on Azalia, and you never mentioned no crack- heads. So, then I checked this one. When I did, I found ole boy back there on the bed. He was rotting out back then." He drew on his cigar again, releasing a plume of fragrant smoke.

"Always remember this, Homie. A wounded animal will always seek familiar ground. I told you, I knew you were running from something. Seeing ole boy put all the pieces of the puzzle together for me. In the beginning me and Miriam sat parked in that old Buick for seven days straight. We camped out two houses down from the house. An idle mind will wonder. Now I still had a lot of dope and Miriam smoked every day.

"I knew if I would've stayed in that spot another day, I would've hit that shit too. I called it a wrap and pulled off, but one of my speakers wasn't working. So, I pulled over and checked it. That's when I found y'all's money.

I knew it was a sign to "do the fool", like you youngsta's say. So, the O.G. got right back on the grind. But four hours of every day I stopped by, hoping you would come. I started to give up hope but then an old buddy of mine, by the name of Voorheeze has a son by the name of DJ. I ran into DJ and he told me a story about a kid that was gonna carjack him if he didn't give him a ride back to Menlo Park. He described everything down to the black .38 special. To me that was a sign to keep waiting." Dirt couldn't believe his ears. Some kind of a God or angel had been looking out for him. Voorheeze was a name that Mama Jennifer used to talk about before she died. Dirt couldn't believe the light skinned nigga that gave him a ride was his son. Dirt would have to track him down.

"Boy, Miriam sure gonna be glad that I finally caught up with you." Chill Will's story finished just as they were pulling up to a big, beautiful mansion.

Dirt was taken aback by the sheer beauty of the colonial style mansion in front of him.

"Who lives here big Homie?" he asked innocently.

Chill Will took a pull on his cigar and looked at Dirt then blew the smoke out the window. He looked at Dirt again and smiled.

"We do."

Dirt's mouth dropped open like the wolf on that Little Red Riding Hood Cartoon.

"Come on, lil Homie." he chuckled as he climbed out the truck.

The front door of the mansion opened, and Dirt saw the most beautiful woman that he had ever laid eyes on step out on the walkway.

"No luck today either, huh?" The look on her face was that of a sad mother who'd lost their child.

Dirt climbed out of the truck and made his way around to the front of the truck where he would be visible.

"Aaaaaaaah!" Miriam screamed at the top of her lungs.

She took off at a dead sprint like Gail Devers. In seconds she'd dropped in front of Dirt screaming.

"Lolo! Oh God, you found him!" She gave him the biggest hug she could muster up.

Immediately a cold chill ran down the base of her spine. She let go of him and looked at him. Something in him had changed. She could feel it. She still did her best to smile.

"Oh Lolo! It's so good to see you!"

"It's Dirt now, Miriam. Lolo is dead." he didn't try to give her a cold stare. It was just on his face.

"Dirt?" she asked, confusion coloring her tone.

"Yeah Dirt. It's short for Dirt Bag." he told her with a nonchalant attitude.

Her senses were right, he had changed. Only Lord knew why, but she could feel the Evil emanating from his pores.

"Well now you heard the man, woman. Gone and give him some room. Coming all out here making a scene like you lost yo cotton picking mind." Although he was fussing, Chill Will had a big smile on his face.

Miriam had been wanting to find him more than Chill after she had gotten clean. Miriam had been addicted to drugs for more than thirty years. Ever since she was a girl a little older than Dirt. Both her and Chill Will knew if it wasn't for Dirt coming into their lives when he did, they both would still be on Skid Row. They attempted to get clean and sober a few times in the past. Each time ended in the same results, failure. Miriam believed the main reason they failed was not having a foundation to build a future on. The money Chill Will, and Dirt Bag hustled, provided this.

"Look at me, fussing like an old mother hen. Come on let's get inside out of this terrible sun." Miriam stood up and the three of them disappeared into the house.

Dave and Poppa went to tend to business.

Inside of the house they washed up, then sat down in front of a meal fit for a king. Dirt went to town like a starving Somalian. Over the meal they made small talk and caught up a little more. It was after his first plate and well into his second, that he told them all the fucked-up shit he had to endure since they'd last seen each other. Miriam cried genuine tears of hurt, and guilt. Knowing that if they'd done more to find him. He would not have gone through any of things that turned him from Lolo to Dirt Bag.

"Sheeeiit, dis muthafucka still alive! Why you ain't knocked his fucking dick in the dirt?" Chill Will wanted to know once Dirt was done talking.

Chill Will was livid.

The sinister look that overcome Dirt's face reminded Miriam of the demons she'd used to see when her family practiced the Black Magic.

"I got something more in store for him, big Homie. Don't you worry bout him." Suddenly Dirt's look changed again. "But first big Homie, I got to find that nigga Von and deal with him."

"Von?" This time it was Chill Will who was surprised. "What chou got to do with that nigga, lil Homie?" Chill Will hoped Dirt wasn't going to say he was throwing in with likes of Von.

Then Chill Will remembered that night so long ago that Von came to the Capri. In order for them to understand he had to tell them what happened to Nyomi that night that Von first brought them to the Capri.

When he was done Miriam was crying even harder and Chill Will had even more respect for his little protégé "Sheeeiit lil Homie, how many bodies yo lil ass got hidden around this muthafucka?" Dirt knew the big Homie wasn't trying to get all up in his business.

"Them the only two so far big Homie."

Dirt didn't see no harm in telling his big Homie the truth. "I'mma save that discussion for when it's just you and me, lil Homie." Chill Will said in humor.

"But for real, lil Homie... I got some information I know you want to hear." The seriousness in Chill Will's tone told Dirt that he needed to pay close attention.

"Alright, big Homie."

"But lil Homie, Von ain't the same Von that you guys were dealing with last year." Dirt wanted to ask what he meant but remembered patience was the key to everything.

"The boy fucked around and teamed up with same people from the other side of the border that got him sitting right with that white girl. He done fucked around and blew up overnight. Shit, lil Homie. Von the man right now and got himself a whole team of killers."

"So, what that mean?" Dirt cut him off.

"It means your job is going to be a whole lot harder than you think." he told him with a serious look on his face.

"Shit, big Homie... ain't nothing been easy for me so far, why should this be any different?" Dirt wasn't being funny. It was the truth.

From everything Chill Will heard from the little nigga he had to admit most grown men would've given up on life or succumbed to the odds a long time ago.

"If anybody could do it, lil Homie. You definitely can." No truer words were ever spoken.

"But lil Homie, I got some information that I know you want to hear. We know where Nyomi's at. She over at Hillcrest Detention Center.

"They ended up giving her three years for the dope that they found her with. Because she wouldn't give up any information on the person that fled out the back window and got away.

"By the time we found her, we tried to get her a good lawyer, but we were too late. A public defender had already railroaded her into taking the deal." Chill Will knew his lil Homie was going to take the news hard.

A lone tear escaped the boundaries of his eyes and fled down his cheek. He wasn't whole without her. The news he heard was like always, bittersweet, a little good a little bad.

He made no attempt to hide his feelings from them. His sweet Nyomi, he'd finally found her. She was being held captive. A prisoner! A slave! And he couldn't do anything to help her. All because he wasn't up on his safety and security.

Guilt tore at his heart adding more pain to all the hurt he'd been through. The loss of Mama Jennifer and everything that followed! It all came out right there at the dinner table.

It was the second time in his life Dirt ever cried. He let it go for all of it!

Miriam got up, walked over, and held him tightly against her bosom. She smelled like Bath & Body Works Cherry Blossom; the same scent Mama Jennifer used to wear. Which made him cry harder.

Thinking of Mama Jennifer, poor Dirt Bag felt like he was having a breakdown of some sort.

Miriam sat holding him for twelve long minutes while he got it all out his system. Chill Will would later think back on this day and realize that this was the day it all began. This would also mark the last time Dirt would cry for a long, long time.

"Can I see her?" was the only question he asked.

"Sure, Baby. I'll take you first thing in the morning. That would be a lovely gift for her especially since tomorrow is Valentine's Day." Miriam assured him.

While he was crying Chill Will got up to make himself a drink and give Dirt some privacy. Thinking on it, he made Dirt one as well. Not only could he use the drink, but he had two bodies under his belt at age 11 he was already grown in Chill Will's eyes.

"Come on and have a drink with me lil Homie. We got some talking to do." he told Dirt as he handed him a glass of Courvoisier.

Dirt grabbed the glass, then kissed Miriam on the cheeks. "Thanks Mama Miriam." he told her and followed Chill Will.

No one saw the tears of joy as they slid down Miriam's cheeks. "Mama Miriam", she loved how that sounded.

CHAPTER TWENTY THREE

Morning could not have come for him soon enough. The night was filled with countless hours of him thinking about Nyomi. Dirt didn't even eat break- fast, he hungered for something that food couldn't fulfill. A taste that breakfast could not satisfy.

The ride out to the facility was a long quiet trip filled with nervous anticipation. Miriam tried to make small talk, but Dirt's one and two-word answers let her know that he wanted to be left alone with his thoughts.

The morning sky was a dark reflection of his soul. Sporadic and unpredictable with threats of a storm hovering on the horizon.

They arrived at the facility and waited for what seemed like forever to get processed. Forever was actually forty-six minutes. Miriam could tell by looking at Dirt that he was a ball of nerves. "Poor little man." She thought to herself. Never before had she seen a more vivid display of pure love on the face of another human being.

Dirt wondered what she would say. How she would feel. Would she still care about him, or would she despise him for her being locked up in here? He'd never seen anyone in jail before. The visiting room wasn't even halfway full. The inmates that he did see looked like grown women, who looked hardened and beaten down by circumstances beyond their control.

Every fifteen seconds, he would look in the direction of the door, waiting for Nyomi to walk through.

Finally, the door did open and in walked his soul mate. Nyomi stood motionless in front of the door for a minute while she scanned the room searching for a familiar face.

"Ny," he whispered as he slowly stood up. Not believing his eyes.

She looked beyond beautiful. Dirt had grown, down in that basement with Terrence's home cooked meals and his workout regimen. Nyomi however had transformed completely.

She'd gone through a growth spurt that made her two inches taller. Putting her at 5'6." The nutritious food put thirty pounds of heartache on her young body. Her Sunkist yellow skin had a sort of cinnamon kiss to it. This wasn't a fifteen-year-old girl. Nyomi was a little woman.

The moment she laid eyes on him; she went through all sorts of emotions. In her mind, she couldn't move a step. In reality, she rushed over into the arms of her man. It all seemed surreal. Nyomi had dreamed of this moment for so long. She could not believe that it was actually happening.

The tears flowed silently down her cheeks, but they flowed non-stop. Their affection drew the attention of every other woman in the room. In the hearts of some of the inmates was pure jealousy. Their boyfriends and husbands had run off long ago. The solid convicts however were happy for her. Everyone knew Nyomi's story and silently in the hearts of the real women. They rooted for her not to end up like them.

The two lovebirds kissed so long and passionately that a few of the ladies were becoming excited just on the familiar memories of their own lost passion.

"Umm...umm. Okay, you two that's enough. Y'all break it up before these people put us out of here before the visit even starts." Miriam joked to get their attention.

They finally broke the embrace and sat down. Never once did they take their eyes off of one another. Nor did they stop holding hands.

Dirt was the first to speak. "Ny, I'm so sorry Bae. Sorry it took so long for me to get to you. Sorry that you're up in here…"

She interrupted "Bae, you got nothing to be sorry about, it wasn't your fault…"

"It was…" he tried to interrupt her, but Nyomi wasn't having it.

"Bae, I knew full well what I was doing. Wasn't none of that your fault. Somebody was going to go down I saw that. I knew that you would be there for me. You'd already showed me that a million times over. I knew you'd be more beneficial out there than me.

"Bae, I was already an emotional wreck! Hell, I was even smoking crack! Calling it medicine because I was too ashamed to call it what it was. If you would've gotten locked up that night instead of me and left me out there with yet another heartache, I would've completely unraveled. I wouldn't have been good enough for me, let alone being able to be there for you.

"I knew you would come. I knew it in my heart. Miriam and Chill Will have kept me company and stocked good with commissary. The only thing I've been missing is you, and now I have you." Dirt just stared at her for a long time. She even talked like a grown woman to him.

"Ny, you know I got here as soon as I could. I just went through some Hollywood Saw IV type of shit, and barely made it out. Naaw… fuck Saw! It was more like some Split kind of shit." The two of them had seen the movie Split together.

"Well Bae, I'm glad you made it and you're here now. But yesterday for that. Let's talk about all of these muscles you got." She changed the subject while stroking his muscled arms. Dirt blushed under his brown skin.

The rest of the visit went as good as the beginning. Seeing the love that shined out of two of them, no one could place an age barrier on love. Their love was easy and genuine.

The only bad thing about the visit was time went by way too fast. It seemed like they were just getting settled when one of the guards announced visitation would be over in ten minutes.

"Fuck! It's time to go already!" It was more of a complaint.

Not a question.

"Tell me about it." Nyomi began to get sad.

"Don't worry Ny. I'mma be here for you. Every visiting day, I'mma be the first nigga in line. When you call Miriam, she'll give you my new phone number. I'm going to get a phone as soon as we leave. And you can bet it's gonna be breaded up for you to call!" Romeo's love for Juliet couldn't have been any stronger than Dirt's love was for Nyomi.

"I love you so much, Bae." The tears began flowing down Nyomi's face again as they stood to leave.

"Don't cry Ny, I got chou Bae." Seeing her cry tore at his heart.

"These tears are joy Bae. Tears of joy." The two of them kissed more deeply than in the beginning. But they didn't press their luck.

Next, Nyomi hugged Miriam good-bye before walking slowly off and approaching the guard who was waiting to escort her back to her cell.

"Hey listen up!" Everyone looked at Dirt startled, even Miriam.

"That's my Queen and future wife right there! Real spit, y'all respect my Queen while I go out here and get her, her throne!" Dirt shouted for all the room to hear.

"Go head then, little Daddy!" One of the girls called out. "Giiiiirl, he gone be a knockout when he gets older, you better watch him!" Another one called out.

"Shiiiit, I might just fuck around and get me a taste of that!" One of the girls she was cool with toyed with her.

"And fuck around and have me back in this bitch for murdering yo ass!" Nyomi joked back.

"You tell her bitch!" Another inmate called out.

Nyomi left the visiting room with tears of joy streaming down her face. But wearing a huge smile on her face as well.

The moment Dirt stepped out of the visiting room he transformed back into the cold-hearted Predator that he needed to become to accomplish all that was on his plate. Miriam saw it but didn't speak on it. She just drove with a smile on her face headed for the phone store. She made a mental note to express her concerns with Chill Will later once they were alone.

**** N. D. ****

Last night in the study while Dirt and Chill Will had their drinks, Chill broke down everything regarding the business to Dirt.

Although coke still sold fairly well in California. The money was in heroin, which was making a big comeback due to so many people being hooked on prescription drugs made from opiates. That and the fact that with El Chapo sitting on ice with the Feds. The new management of the Sina Loa Cartel was allowing certain buyers to get their hands - on kilos of pure Fentanyl. You could turn one kilo of heroin into two thousand kilos.

Fentanyl was extremely potent.

Now, Chill Will wasn't quite yet one of those lucky customers that could buy the Fentanyl. But as it turned out Miriam had an older brother named Kaveh that was one of those privileged few who could get access.

The family was so thankful for Chill Will getting their Miriam off drugs that they offered him anything he wanted free of charge. Her family was into drugs and guns heavily.

Chill Will couldn't see himself getting something for helping his woman get better, so he turned down the offer. After one long talk with Kaveh one night about Miriam and his future, the two men reached an agreement.

Chill Will took all the money that was made off the kilos of coke. Both his and Dirt's and got a good deal on three kilos of premium grade-A heroin along with a kilo of pure Fentanyl fronted to him at a price tag of a quarter million dollars. Chill Will didn't need a chef to fuck up his life savings. He whipped it up himself.

It took him three and a half weeks, four cement mixers, and all the raw materials he would need to turn the three kilos of heroin and a kilo of Fentanyl into almost five hundred kilos of some fire fucking smack.

One phone call to his nephew, Blood James, and his team was assembled. Dave and Poppa were two of the most vicious, money getting young muthafuckas he'd ever met.

Chill Will literally went from a nothing ass crackhead, to "Don" status overnight. In a move that would've shocked any money-getting hustler. Chill Will told Dirt he could have any position on the team he wanted.

Including the head. Shockingly Dirt turned him down.

Telling his mentor that the day would come when he would come for his rightful place on the throne. But today wasn't that day. He had a plan, and he was going to stick with it.

Dirt wanted to climb up through the ranks from the very bottom so that he would be familiar with and able to master every aspect of a machine. By the time he reached the top, Dirt would have assembled his own team.

Chill Will understood it and respected it. If he handed the reins over to Dirt. On the surface his team would honor it, but underneath they would always be loyal to Chill Will until the day that they began doubting him for handing the keys to the kingdom over.

For Chill Will to make the gesture and offer it, showed his level of love and respect he had for his young protégé. He also told Dirt he had $500,000 that belonged to him.

Now Dirt loved the sound of that but asked the big Homie to do him a favor and hold it for a little while. He didn't have a problem with that.

After finishing up all the business with one another. Dirt had to go tend to his business. Poppa drove Dirt back to Menlo Park. He dropped him off in the alleyway behind the laundromat. Poppa went down memory lane for a moment because this was his old stomping grounds as well.

While Chill Will and Miriam got ready for their Valentine's date. Dirt was getting ready for a date of his own. He walked into the taco shack and ordered his normal four tacos and a super burrito, then waited for the woman to bring it to him. He sat at his usual table with the usual scowl on his young face. As she brought him his food the woman couldn't help but wonder why such a young boy would have such a serious look on his face all the time.

"Here you go." she said as she placed the food on the table in front of him.

"Senora, I need to speak with you, un momento." he told her in a low voice.

"I'm sorry, but we are very busy today. Maybe next time."

She turned to walk away but then stood still when she heard him say something again in a low voice.

"Excuse me?" she said once she turned back around.

Could this little boy be playing some kind of cruel joke on her? Was he just being nasty? She wondered.

"I said your life is in danger." he spoke again in his low steely voice.

He gestured towards the empty seat across from him "Please, five minutes is all I ask."

"Carlos!" Esmeralda called over to the man behind the counter. After telling him something in Spanish she took a seat. She didn't speak a word.

It only took two minutes for him to tell her the tale of that night he was outback and overheard the phone call Hector had made. And to give her the details of him stealing the black bag and what its contents were.

When Dirt finished, he gestured to the bag on the seat next to her, telling her to open it. Esmeralda didn't know why but she believed the little boy without even looking in the bag. When she did her heart skipped a beat. Inside was the dossier that was in the bag were photos of her along with instructions. They were written in her husband's handwriting.

She sat quietly for a long-time digesting and dissecting the information. She couldn't believe it. So that's what had happened to Felipe. All this time she'd thought he'd run away with another. Now she knew Hector had killed him.

When she looked at Dirt her icy eyes matched his cold stare. They were both devoid of emotion. Empty like the deep blue ocean.

"So, what do you want?" she had to be careful, the little boy could be a part of some elaborate scheme by her husband as well.

For the first time his facial expression changed. His head was bowed. He was looking at her out the top of his eyes with an evil smile on his face.

"Simple, Senora, I wanna kill him."

**** N. D. ****

Dirt made sure to lock the back door behind him. It sort of felt weird walking into that house of his own free will. He made his way down to the basement.

The foul smell of feces and urine assaulted his nose. Musk was attempting to join the odorous assault. When he made it to the bottom of the staircase, he saw Terrence balled up on the floor in fear. He thought Dirt had come down there to hurt him again.

"I brought you something to eat." Dirt tossed the long bag with the burritos over to Terrence.

He hadn't eaten in days. Hunger overpowered fear and he tore into the burritos. Dirt sat down on the last stair watching Terrence eat his food. So many thoughts raced through his head. Thoughts of all the cruel and fucked up things that he wanted to do to Terrence. Oh, the pleasure he would receive from torturing Terrence.

"Be leery of the one who comes bearing gifts, for he is the one who will mislead you with his wicked ways."

Dirt was looking directly at Terrence, but it was Mama Terry that was looking back at him, and it was her who spoke.

"And woe to them that held my children captive for I shall blot their entire existence out from the world."

She was hunched over looking at Dirt heinously while quoting Scripture. Ranting and raving about this and that.

Dirt's cell phone began ringing. Only three people had the number. He prayed it was her.

"Hello."

"This is IC Solutions, you have a prepaid call from, "It's Ny, Bae." Who is an inmate at Hillcrest Detention Center, your trust account balance is $50.00, the price of this call will be five cents per minute. The time limit for this call is fifteen minutes. To accept this call press 5 now...."

"Hey Bae!" Nyomi shouted into the phone.

"What's up, Bae?" he closed his eyes picturing her bright smile.

"You can't keep us forever you little Dirt Bag! We will be free and when we do…." Dirt was ignoring the rants of Mama Terry. "Bae, what in the world is that?" It sounded purely evil to Nyomi. "Ny, hold on for one second, Bae." Dirt put the phone on mute.

He wanted to do even more to Mama Terry than he had done to Terrence. He looked at her with hatred burning brightly in his eyes.

"I am Legion…"

"You're dead now, bitch." Dirt loved the way his new 9mm he had purchased from Chill Will felt in his hands as he blew that evil bitch's head off. Sure, he wanted to torture both her and Terrence in countless ways, but fuck that, he had shit to do. He could not waste time playing games.

Heading back up the stairs he unmuted the phone. "Ny?"
"Yeah, Bae." she answered.

"Sorry about that."

"It's okay. What was that bae?" she asked for the second time.

"That was the devil, bae." he answered her as he closed the door to the basement and that chapter of his life.

Until a Predator is born……

THANKS!!

A tremendous amount of thanks and gratification goes out to any and everyone who has ever given me a reason. Rather you hated on me, lied on me, abused my trust and friendship, told me what I couldn't do, doubted me, or tried to break me. You've given me a reason and I thank you.

If you motivated and inspired me, attempted to push me, taught, and showed me, gave me a chance, believed when no one else did (including myself), didn't question, judge nor ridicule, but nourished, helped, and molded me...... You most definitely gave me a reason and I Love You for it.

For my destination is greatness and my reason is I can. I can reach my goals and achieve my dreams, fully see reality along the way. I began this journey with one supporter, Lesia. She believed in me when even I doubted myself. Now I have many followers and supporters. If all of you, are all I ever touch, then I am grateful, and I thank God for you. However, if God shall permit, I will reach the hearts of millions, and I shall do it with the love, support, and belief of all my readers and supporters and I thank each and every one of you!!!!!!

KHATARI

Author Khatari on Facebook

Join My Facebook Groups:

Khatari's Pen is Lethal & Khatari's Korner

Dirt Bag 2: A Predator is Born

PRELUDE

Thunder erupted violently in a loud roar off in the distance. The sound was so ferocious that it shook the earth miles below. Surely, the Gods were beyond angry with man and they chose tonight to act out their vengeance. Nickel-sized raindrops pelted every surface, assaulting everything in its path, having no consideration for anything or anyone. He stood still, buried deep within his own thoughts as the raindrops pummeled against his body. His eyes transfixed on a sight only he could see. A vision, a place and time, only he remembered. Dirt Bag's body was nearly frozen due to the cold, rain, and wind. Yet, he was oblivious to his present perils. He was lost in a self-made time capsule from hell. The gruesome acts that took place inside the house he watched would forever haunt his young mind. The images that would fester and give birth to a predator. Unresolved pain would breed and groom the predator into something that even the predators of the night feared.
An Apex Predator!

After staring for a long time, Dirt Bag blinked, and his vision focused on the present. The image of the outside of the house in front of him replaced the horrors being chained like a rabid animal and tortured like a prisoner of war. For the first time, Dirt Bag noticed the rain drops as they hit his goose-bumped riddled body. The wild wind bit his exposed flesh and only now did it register in his mind. Slowly, a smile formed and spread across his face. A sinister look formed in his eyes. Had someone walked by at that exact moment, that look would put the fear of God into them. They were the malevolent eyes of someone with a bloodlust. They were the eyes of the Devil. They were the eyes of Dirt Bag.
THE PREDATOR.

Made in the USA
Monee, IL
21 January 2022

89486262R00118